Splashes from Life

Splashes *from* Life

DR. BRAJENDRA K JHA

PARTRIDGE

Print information available on the last page.

To order additional copies of this book, contact
Partridge India
000 800 10062 62
orders.india@partridgepublishing.com

www.partridgepublishing.com/india

Contents

Foreword

These stories tell what happens in everyone's life when he experiences good and bad, happiness and sadness, criticism and appreciation. It becomes almost devastating when very close person give blow mild or severe. One has to bear all and continue living. He doesn't give up and that's interesting about life.

Dr Brajendra K Jha

Ignorant

1

'Son I love you so much. Do you know how much I suffered before you were born at age of just seventeen? I was admitted frequently in hospital for blood transfusion. Your Daddy was always absent and my mother took me to hospital in rickshaw on rough roads. I was scared when doctor threatened about abortion. I was not getting good food and even milk was not available regularly. Mother cried in night and spent every minute with me. Other family members kept normal and unconcerned. They said plainly that I was not their responsibility.' Rajani talked over long distance call to Karan her only son.

'Why are you telling me these details and what I should do about it now?' Karan replied without any feelings. She was in tears for long and cursed son for harshness. Husband was a bit crazy and never respected her feelings and softness. He felt ladies are only crying lot and whenever they find themselves alone, they preferred to cry. Their storage of tears was big and generation was speedy which required frequent unloading. Thereafter, they became harshest possible individual and could tear apart anyone who tried to clash.'Nature has made woman only like this; once they are soft like ice-cream and next moment sharp and tough like thorns in big rose plants. This contrast was interesting but for some very painful.' Rohit expressed when unhappy with behavior of wife Rajani. He thought that his fate was hard not knowing that majority population experienced same. Rajani was shocked with talk of son and started crying. Her husband died few years back and she managed alone. She never agreed to stay with son. One reason was uncompromising nature of daughter-in-law. Karan married Lucia while in training in Paris sent by company. He met her in park one Sunday and got attracted by her beauty. She became close fast and allowed Karan to have all possible pleasure without restriction. She also went to a motel to sleep with him after only a few days and he was obliged to marry her later. His emotional weakness came to the fore and he couldn't back out like many others in affairs.

Lucia was selfish and wanted to live alone for avoiding checks or restrictions. Rajani tried to teach Indian culture and manners which she disliked. Now Rajani stayed alone passing time with friends. She had no hobby and one habit of writing in magazines and papers also was lost when she was unable to concentrate. It started right from day when husband died who inspired. She was confined for long hours. She came out of apartment once a week to buy provisions and rested for whole day. She missed food many days and disengaged her full time maid. She worked in house to pass time and speed of work gradually came down. She lost vigor and strength. Her friends also found her company boring and stopped visiting her. Once or twice some old male acquaintances dropped on her door to enquire and they were driven away in harshest possible manner.

Many times people thought her to be dead. Charming and outspoken Rajani was a past in society. Her eyes were sunk in eye pits, her rosy lips got black and hair became thin and shabby. Her husband was proud of long hair and many days he washed and combed after rinsing for hours. He smelled her head and kissed face several times getting intoxicated with smell in head. Thereafter most days they made prolonged love and didn't bother to reply door bells. Once or twice their important mails were returned which Rohit got from post office after hours of chasing and often bribing. He never felt bad about it.

'Why you get mad after washing my hair so painfully?' Rajani asked.

'This looks more attractive than Romila's; most popular film actress. We have always been seeing all her releases. After returning from cinema I never allowed you to be away and we slept for long without food many nights.' He replied.

'This shows you have gone crazy and one day your boss is going to kick you out.' She warned.

'Why you say so?' He sounded worried.

'Romila is name of his wife. He will doubt you having affair with her, if he listens all that you say to me.' She reminded.

'Are you going to tell him?' He joked.

'Yes if you don't stop over pampering me. Even otherwise I am getting thinner and you force me to be hungry for many nights. My mother said that one loses flesh in quantum of a lovely sun bird if food is not taken in night. Additionally you make me to play almost whole night.' She said with smile.

'You also like this and don't deny.' He advanced but stopped.

'One day I am going to kill you for all this mischief and no one will know.' She was speaking with artificial anger.

'I shall be too glad to die with your hand. But I shall be back to torture you in different ways.' Rajani heard him talk last. Next day Rohit met with serious accident and expired. Her curse took his life and Karan is avenging and fulfilling promise made by him.

2

Rajani started crying and stopped after many hours. She got up and ate bread sandwich, an easier preparation and fill up hungry stomach. One day suddenly she met Rajesh in market place. This was a chance when he was in town for some work. He was her boy friend in college and both fell for each other and decided to marry.

Luck was not with them as father of Rajesh asked him to go outside country to take care of business which was facing problems. It happened suddenly and he was not able to explain any detail to Rajani. She went to see him off in railway station when informed by him. His parents were standing nearby and she couldn't dare to talk. He only signaled to be in touch and marry after returning back. This is what she understood. This never happened and one day parents got her married to Rohit. She objected and told mother about her choice that rejected it as fantasy.

'Rajani good boys are difficult to find. Rohit is well behaved and also moneyed and can take care of all your needs.'

'What will happen to child I am carrying from Rajesh?'

'Either get rid or hide it from Rohit. Firstly you were foolish to get pregnant and now you are asking me what to do. It will be difficult for him to find origin. You must act very romantic and devoted from day one and engage him. Rest all will be set. Never tell anyone either in family or outside.' Mother tutored.

'I won't be able to do so. Better I should end my life.' She replied.

'Like many other fools like you and get publicity to give us bad name.' Mother toughened talk.

She rushed to bed room and as usual cried for many days. Mother kept consoling and convincing. She took help from her two close friends who experienced similar situations but got free in clinics.

3

Rajani finally obeyed mother and acted as advised. Karan was born and big celebration happened. Rajani forgot her previous love and became true wife of husband who loved deeply. He was lost in her eyes which wanted to tell some story and was sleepy even in day time. This he treated as special feature who otherwise talked poetic and recited verses from books. She wrote poems and Rohit promoted them. She gradually got fame in literary world and was honored. She attended gathering and sang sweet songs which normally end with message of sadness. Rohit was afraid of losing her and stopped attending gathering of poets. Rajani started shrinking and remained confined to home. She didn't entertain visitors and tried to avoid his friends also. He couldn't pressurize and made excuse of bad health most of time. None thought otherwise and advised names of medical specialists for check up and necessary treatment.

Karan grew in such depressed environment and became serious at early age. He turned philosophical and debated with mother in harsh tongue. Once or twice Rohit banged him when Rajani objected. She considered self responsible for whatever was happening. They decided to send Karan to boarding school to have free atmosphere. He did well in school and also became a good sportsman. He never wanted to come home. Father brought him to see mother only for few days and took him on outing during vacation. Rajani didn't want to travel and stayed at home. Karan lost interest in mother and thought her to be highly selfish. He never kept any photograph of mother and many times told friend that mother was no more. They expressed sympathy but never probed.

4

Karan successfully completed his college and went to do IT course and got job in campus interview. Company sent him for further training to Paris and left wife with mother for learning house hold jobs. Karan never informed parents and secretly married. Rajani tried to teach Lucia but she was not interested. She liked luxury and company of boys in absence of husband. She didn't allow and forced her to remain at home.

Lucia was not happy and within few days opposed mother-in-law in everything that she said. She started behaving abnormal and always did things which upset

Rajani. She one day banged her when and called her names. Rajani couldn't tolerate and pushed her out from house. She remained in street for whole night and was allowed to return next morning. Karan became very angry with mother. He decided not to stay with her anymore in future. Karan returned and heard about it from wife who was in tears while narrating. He couldn't control anger and insulted mother. Instantly they left home and stayed in hotel for few days before leaving for US, his place of new placement. Rohit came to know and tried to pacify but didn't insist. He was greatly pained with insult of wife. He only informed wife about Karan and Lucia leaving for US on being posted by company. Rajani was greatly shocked and knew she wouldn't be meeting son any more.

'I know that lady has snatched my son. Firstly you sent Karan away from me for education and now Lucia has taken control. It is good and he deserved this. After all he was not your son.' Rajani confessed.

'What are you talking?' Rohit asked.

'I am telling you truth. You married me when I was pregnant from Rajesh whom I loved. His parents opposed and sent him to US for business. I don't know why people go to US leaving family forever. They all become so selfish in life.' She talked in temper.

Rohit was shocked to learn truth about Karan and became quiet. He felt ditched by wife and her reality was something different. His whole life looked to him unwanted. He was lost and walked out of house. It was evening and roads were dark due to load shedding. He was hit by a racing car which fled away. None bothered to pick him up to carry to hospital. All were afraid of callousness of police who involved people unnecessarily to hide ineffectiveness of force. They bothered only for bosses and political people and attacked general mass for no reasons. He was taken to hospital by some old people in car and was declared dead. Police harassed those people for many days but could do no harm. They wanted money which was refused.

This news was given to Rajani by police who was nonreactive. Finally neighbors did honor of last rites but she didn't move out of home. She had turned stone faced and skeleton of human body with flesh and bones. One looking at her was shocked and recalled how a talented woman was changed into this shape. She was mainly responsible and she didn't compromise with conditions while husband tried to serve her in best way. She gradually changed once again to live with all around. She responded with very few words and gave feeble smile to some who cut jokes with her. It became mystery how transformation started. It was found that she lived with one young woman Misa who came as tourist and was left alone by group travelling to other places in northern hills. She was from Kazakistan and spoke little bit of English. It forced Rajani to talk in English and communicate.

'Madam I have made tea for you. Would you like some biscuits or any other snack?' Girl said.

'No give me snacks and you eat biscuits with tea. Give me more sugar and milk. Light tea is not good for me.' Rajani said.

'What you will like in lunch?' Girl asked.

'Rice fried Dal with onion and tomato.' She replied.

Rajani started getting back food taste which she lost all these days despite good attention from Rohit. Misa was engaged by him only who slept also with him replacing sick wife many nights. Once it was revealed by her to Rajani.

'Did you enjoy sleeping with him? I never found him good. It was bad and remorseful. He was having some bad habits to treat harshly with no affection or love. It was all mechanical and forceful.' Rajani asked

'Yes madam. He was not good when in excitement and efforts were required. He had told me about this while fixing payment. He also told that after your death he will marry formally to make me his wife.'

'He was so mean still you accepted.' Rajani was anguished.

'He was not mean but a sick man and you forced this in him.' Girl replied.

Rajani was angered and hit her with empty tea cup. Misa bent to avoid injury. Rajani became more accessible. One day Misa informed that her friends were back. She left to go. She was paid all dues and also some new clothes. Misa cried before leaving her alone. She couldn't stay back because her parents awaited arrival of daughter. She never told them the life she spent last two months.

5

Surprisingly Rajani further normalized and started mixing with friends as if some bad curse was over. All welcomed this change and she joined in kitty parties as usual. She won in games and made money. It was in one such party that Rajesh appeared. He came to drop his sister before going to club. She saw Rajesh and spoke to him.

'When did you come back from US? Why you never contacted me from there? It is not costly. My son at times talks to me but not his wife.'

'I came a month back. My sister told me when you changed to be normal after losing husband in accident.'

'Who is your sister?' Is it Ruby who looks like you?

'Ruby is naughty and always keeps demanding gifts. This time I have given her new car.'

'Is that the red one? I like that color.'

'If you want I can get you one as gift.'

'No that will be burden for me. I can't drive and also can't afford a driver."

'You take me as driver for life."

'What do you mean? Where is your wife?'

'I never married. My father bluffed in beginning and afterwards I refused to marry.'

'It means there is still place for me in your house. I have become so repulsive you could reject me.'

'Rajani love is never rejected. You are still in heart and come to my home.'

'What will happen to this flat?'

'It will be made guest house for company and you will be fully compensated.'

'Are you definite what you are talking? Don't dump me afterwards as men usually do after enjoying briefly and losing interest.'

'Your eyes are my attraction. Eyes never fade and remain charming at all age.'

Finally Rajani married Rajesh and told him about Karan. Karan lived in Switzerland now and worked for a Swiss company as head of administration. Lucia was still with him and they had a daughter now grown up but unmarried. Rajani told him about Karan who was his son only. Rohit was told but same day met with accident and died.

'No you don't know. Rohit told me about your being pregnant before marriage. On my request he allowed you to carry child. We met at intervals whenever I came on business tour and met in hotel. He was very generous and loved you more than me.'

'You people used me for your pleasure. Now again you are keeping me for self happiness. That's the reason my son doesn't recognize rather hates me.'

'Not really for this but for your harsh nature and rude behavior.'

Rajani asked Rajesh to call Karan and Lucia home. She wanted to seek pardon from two. Lucia must by now feeling motherhood and should behave normal. Both came one day after many months and Rajani was shocked to see Misa in place of Lucia.

'When you married Karan? She asked.

'After death of Lucia while giving birth to child. Karan was depressed and wanted to end life. I had gone with parents on tour to Switzerland and stopped him from jumping into lake to end life. It took big effort to get him on track. On advice of parents we got married. The child stays with us only.' Misa gave details.

'How you agreed to sleep with Rohit who was father of Karan?'

'You are wrong. Rajesh is father of Karan as told by you now. I did so with your knowledge and to save your husband who was going to end his life.'

'How can you say this now? Why you didn't tell me then?'

'Rohit stopped me due to your poor health. He also thought you will become normal by shock after revelation. But he died in accident before that. Otherwise also we never slept together. We acted to give this impression to you in particular.' Rajani became silent again. Rajesh took her to best hospital where she couldn't get cured. Every month she was diagnosed new disease as if all illness waited to appear. She donated her body to hospital and finally died after six months sickness. Karan, Misa and Rajesh started living together. Rajesh changed place to forget memory of Rajani which was mixed with different feelings. Love and hate cycle worked constantly in his mind.

They went on excursion with others to Europe that included a cruise trip. One night Rajesh jumped into sea in dead of night. Next day it was too late to find body. Karan was informed who shed few drops of tear and cursed self being born in such troublesome family. He never liked mother and continued to do so after her death also. He had full sympathy with Rajesh who acted like father all time and protected him from dangers and getting lost in crowd.

Eminence

1

Bhuvan reached home after long stay out of country and it didn't take much time to get free from all pains in company of Sudha, his wife and son who was extremely naughty. He disturbed a lot in night whenever he got romantic and felt, "Why this fellow has arrived so disturb. He could have waited for more days.""Why are you rude to son? Go and sleep in next room and spare us. This rejection set him right. This place and work are terrible and there is no life for human beings where work prevails everywhere. Go and see state government officers who really enjoy life," said wife in bitter tone. Bhuvan preferred to keep quiet for peace and kept playing with kid to make wife happy and smiling and got benefit of warm hug and long kiss on both cheeks. "What this fellow must have thought about us?" She thought later.

On returning to work place, he was placed in Engineering Department and made in-charge of Bearing Cell. This was an insignificant department with three persons reporting him including one supervisor and one Diploma Engineer, which was utterly frustrating. He decided to start construction of house to compensate for failure of father to have own home. He believed in using opportunity and time. It never meant negligence of duties. In office he prepared Manual on installation, upkeep and selection of bearings. This became reference document for maintenance engineers. It was an important guideline document for purchase department because of its clarity, and even non-technical persons could use document with ease. Later he found that copy of manual was taken by other companies as it covered comparative detail of different manufacturers. He visited plants of bearing manufacturers who sought his guidance on setting production lines. He was sought after person on bearing issues. Bhuvan was called to resolve case of bearing of Mill Stand which broke down in operation and replacement became a critical decision. Available bearings were pitted due to sea water during shipment and nobody wanted to take risk in deciding to use. He inspected all and suggested ways to use them.

The crisis was over. He was amused to find that how scared were senior level people to take critical decision. In fact one senior commented that he had written a suicide note and may lose job any time. It was a culture of "Prolonged Discussions" and "Decision Paralysis" restricting growth of company. Bhuvan was tough and daring in eyes of colleagues and friends. His risk taking capabilities enhanced with passage of time but career stagnated. This he understood when no promotion was granted His working in Bearings Cell earned him good reputation due to hard work and readiness to accept challenges. Construction of house was planned well and few could know when he visited site and how he managed second front. This became his style to manage multiple problems simultaneously. Even boss could not know when house was completed and he started residing there. He didn't want to publicize and avoided house warming party. His second son was born in new house and his parents joined. He was under tremendous financial pressure and fund crunch. His career was dragging despite sincere and hard work. He got promotion to next position in extended but still unrecognized department. He worked out total system of working and made it significant for others to copy system and control method. He now became cooperative and developed understanding with heads and helped in meeting Production Targets. It was not easy to get through impediments in career growth and next promotion came after eight years in same department without additional responsibility. He felt low and disgraced and extremely frustrated. He planned and studied MBA through a distance learning program. He started lecturing in training center to earn additionally and made life easier. His family burden increased when his sons started going to school. He was selected trainer to train executives in "New Appraisal System". It was an opportunity to mix with senior executives at plant level and corporate level including Chairman. His interest in HR grew while being trained as a trainer on appraisal system. He enjoyed conducting sessions and every time improved his delivery in Training Sessions. He became sought after faculty being invited by other plants. He trained both executives and non-executives, and training department always tried to engage him for sessions. It became competitive when others got interested to teach. He withstood and continued because of PGDM qualification. Participants liked to attend his lectures which were informative and useful in practice. Later he proved to be a good teacher in Management. Bhuvan was also active in Social Service and spent many Sundays in service projects. Sudha supported as it was a forum which changed her personality to be open to outside world. She made friends from different regions and social settings and refined her thought process and living habits. He was conscious not to go down in performance with multiple activities. He developed working system involving all subordinates and distributed responsibility. Reporting system was set and all followed strictly. Not even once he failed in briefing seniors on any matter in work. Management generally never recognized this aspect of working and didn't give any special protection considering it to be normal and routine. He found it better to have lower publicity to keep off and remain normal and safe. His learning about personnel management working and dealing with workforce got polished. Now he started appreciating why management fails in avoiding conflict and unrest in organization serving Union interests more than desired. These experiences became useful in working when he could handle different types of people with success. This didn't spare him from woes as many took it personal and tried to create controversy. He faced challenges on personal life which he faced boldly and without bowing down to pressures.

He was careful enough to solve problems and issues only in interest of department and organization and never tried to take personal advantage. In fact this proved to be strength all time and he faced most labor problems with confidence and dignity. He was always worried for future and he consulted astrologers to put on number of rings on fingers. He also studied this subject and made astrological predictions and impressed many. He mastered art of suppressing feelings. He was upset about career and all factors were adverse. He kept cool and contacted anyone who could possibly help. Many were amused by situation and suggested actions like making representations to higher ups. His good sense prevailed to contain difficult time and waited for change to happen in normal course. He often turned poetic and expressed:

Time does care for all but unknown,
Things happened reasons not known,
Unknown wind pushes one to move,
It is destined for all reasonable ends.

2

Bhuvan was highly frustrated with work content and felt that his talents were underutilized. He started talking under this influence and in serious tone, Working long years in department was monotonous and boring. He sought some change in area of work and job and department. He made attempts to change outside organizations, but could hardly find any good position. There was stiff competition everywhere and incumbents could prevent outsiders to enter. Travelling to different places for change became only a pleasure trip. He was finding it additionally difficult because of family commitments, a well settled life, and, no enough gain in terms of money in new jobs being offered. Finally he decided to manage change within with higher responsibility and better career prospect. Such opportunity arrived with the arrival of new head from other place. He was a person with high reputation for hard work and also believing in organizational changes with good and capable persons. It was a difficult to seek change of job and department from him, but it was set in mind. Once in the past he sought change in department in past and he experienced regret, sarcasm, pains and bitterness. He was down for long with injury of sentiments. He regained his courage and move. Bhuvan continued despite failure of many attempts. He found a friend in office of head of plant who helped him to get an interview. He was asked to solve his critical problems faced daily in operating departments. He took up challenge and untiringly worked for six months giving results while running own department. It was a peculiar situation when he was reprimanded by immediate boss several times. He tolerated those and continued. Changes in departments in general were done by senior persons on their sweet will and not on requests. I didn't fall in category of favorites. He only maintained high level of personal performance to keep good reputation this was his only strength. This prevented colleagues to become adversary.

My friend advised me to wait for the opportunity. He met him quite often to chat and gather information on plant working which many times proved useful work. He helped him to gather information on working in many cases which was useful to them. One day he received an urgent call from office to tell that management was looking for a person to head foundry which was performing bad. All were being criticized for poor working and getting nasty communications. Bhuvan was excited and met Chief within few days to inform readiness to take responsibility to improve working of department in shortest possible time. There were some internal resistances. Old guards and their supporters also tried to create hurdle and decision was delayed. Finally he was placed, but his immediate boss became adversary for him. He took all staff and subordinates into confidence. He was more anxious about workman and supervisors who delivered results. He took longer time to find opposing executives by directly talking to them and assigning tasks. He regularly checked personally and emphasized not to fail. Initial few months proved difficult but still monthly production increased. He congratulated concerned officers and demoralized who performed deliberately low. The game got opened and in some months action was taken against poor performers.

Bhuvan was habitually prompt and on reports about problem reached spot before anyone. He never bothered his seniors in odd hours. Their usual practice of playing "Hot Potato Game' became ineffective in which, they tossed problems to each other continuously and passed valuable working hours. They tried to avoid decision making or sharing responsibility.

3

Superintendent of foundry liked to spend time in long meetings. Bhuvan was posted as Manager to take control. He was promoted as Superintendent which was most desirable happening in his career. His learning in few months before placement was helpful to make an early and fast beginning. He openly sought help from all. Working in shop was quite challenging as he had limited knowledge of metallurgy as mechanical engineer. He referred to books to update his knowledge and also journals from central library regarding working. Managing experience of people two decades became a big strength and potent tool. His management education also became big support in managing shop floor. He found that sensible approach in solving men related problems was most important in working. A systematic and sympathetic but fast handling was key tool success. Bhuvan started systematically firstly by assigning definite task to shift managers to increase production. They were also directed on matter of disciplining workers and staff in a fair manner without tolerating any unwanted actions. Time keeping by all was enforced strictly and all were asked to attend shop floor problems directly. System was developed to organize activities and it was monitored regularly by controlling officers keeping them updated. Human factor was most important consideration when operating shop to fulfill challenging target set by him. Managers were encouraged to take interest in human factors from all angles and remain proactive. Initially they slipped because they never believed these softer ways of looking on work force. They normally considered them as persons reporting to work according to their desires. None was free to decide and work. Bhuvan convinced them to allow people to be free to perform and assist them in optimizing results.

This type of work culture started giving positive results and confidence of employees increased who now wanted more challenging targets. The key factor of teamwork was emphasized in every meeting and all were asked to redress complaints with mutual discussion to ensure success of leader. All effective managers came up with several solutions to problem in an open house discussion for selection and implementation of best one and where correction was possible during process. Manager was to involve person from other related department in working group which helped him to achieve production target. Bhuvan decided to ensure Managers were made responsible to educate and train employees under them so that new methods with changed technology could be implemented. Long experience on job may not always be a valid experience. This also interfered in good interpersonal relation. What was important Total Personality of individual manager, and not only his educational qualification, family or social background and influencing manners? These feats could happen sometimes but cannot be relied in longer perspective of organization. An unsatisfactory interpersonal relation proved to be unproductive and sometimes dangerous for good functioning organization making its life shorter. Maintenance in production shop got secondary consideration and was normally area where production managers and supervisors tried to avoid and stick to their production plans. The works manager has to keep up morale of persons working in such secondary function including the inspection group. Good interpersonal relation not only built working environment, but it also shielded it from any criticism from external environment.

4

A happy but disciplined team can only serve any organization for long when work pressures do not generate unwanted tensions. In area of human behavior he found that only 'logical decision' might not always be correct decision. This depended on situation when one made decisions that involved humans. There were increased numbers of cases where a management decision to improve efficiency by controlling labor costs caused production disruption. In some cases such action brought enterprise to standstill. People in production line maintained short sightedness for immediate results. Small favors were given without much thinking and ignoring implications on rules or practices. These all became root causes of major industrial unrest when they came forward with long charter of demands quoting precedence.

All questions on industrial relations, quality control, resources availability, good understanding with consumer departments hovered in Bhuvan's mind and he was engrossed to improve production and achieve rated capacity as promised. A good communication system was set up for regular feedback and information on progress. Reports in written memoranda, notices, circulars, and office orders, minute of meetings were part of communication. But these were subtle types of communication. Informal conversation was set in working and many times proved more effective. Communication network in shop was improved. What was happening in particular section of department? What decisions were taken in coordination meeting? How decisions were implemented? How workmen executives were reacting to changes brought in? Why productivity was not picking up? What was progress in breakdown jobs? How many reported for duty on bund day? What safety measures were taken as per factory rules?Leadership became most critical in department when new technology was implemented and structures of organization remained unchanged. Bhuvan influenced behavior of people to ensure development of new method and this required true leadership quality with knowledge, skill and positive attitude. People were forced into new order by creating challenging situations within organization. In a working plant this type of situations were created to break monotony as well as to give an opportunity to working people to experiment with new ideas. Unrest appeared from time to time. Bhuvan never thought that total absence of conflict may end in death of organization. Human beings cannot remain calm all time when working in groups where clash of interest, aspirations, desires, demands were common feature. The effectiveness of shift coordination meeting was important. Incentive if not communicated and explained carefully posed prolonged disturbance. Only written scheme may not be enough and sufficient explanation to workers was equally important. Adequacy of system, appropriateness and its role in carrying out plan and strategy were important aspects in communication. The criteria were soundness of Products for prolonged service life and lower consumption in steel production. This was factor in calculation of production cost of steel matching to international norm. Initially it appeared to be simple but ultimately became important factor and serious consideration.

Working of foundry and achievement of rated capacity had spiraling effect. It was subsequently observed that demoralized group never thought in terms of reaching rated capacity and concluded that designers were at fault. The change was initiated by saying that it was wrong to challenge designer as he included factor of safety in designs and cushion for several unknown factors influencing rate of production circumstances. All efforts should be made to reach rated capacity and it was always possible. One has to approach to situation with confidence to achieve goal of production solving problems without delays. This happened and shop achieved rated output level in 15 months. One measure introduced was adherence to quality parameters without relaxation. Quality Circles were formed in all sections and all were trained by certifying agency recruited for this. They developed system for all sections and tested on pilot programs before introducing on shop floor. This was method to involve workers and supervisors in continuous improvement in all areas of operations.

Suggestions were invited for introducing modifications and changes at moderate cost and prompt implementation with economical use of inputs, spares etc. Managers used to compete in cost cutting and faster implementation as they could witness changes mainly due to their efforts and shop hummed with activities. Breakdowns reduced and maintenance needs declined and shop was full of finished products. Higher goals could never be achieved in past and no appreciation was given for good performance or recognition at year end in writing or reward. Quality played important role in changing attitude of people towards job performance and same could be heard in social circles. Foundry shop was using high grade technology with complex metallurgical process. Use of sand, chemicals, hot-metal and various other ingredients were environment spoilers. Health hazards were many and they needed prompt attention. Safety was important consideration as heavy duty cranes were operated in the shop handling heavy loads while people down below was engaged in work. Movement of materials was planned and many of hazardous operations were done with great care not to injure man or equipment. Sand dust could affect health and person could become sick with ordinary cold to serious chest infection. The dust extraction system was made effective. Starting quality circles gave ideas for development. All took challenge to implement schemes funded by management. It started attracting visitors which gave positive vive to employees who could appreciate importance of environment. The changed management introduced programs which helped indirectly productivity improvement. People reduced lunch recess; and returned to work place fast. The WOW factor came to play. A healthy management trend got set for all to see and appreciate as absenteeism reduced greatly.

5

In shop he started practicing ethical working each and every department and sections. Production reporting was made regular and factual. Quality parameters were adhered to in all work practices. Honest feedback was gathered from customers. Raw material supplies checks were strengthened and maintenance was done with all sincerity to reduce breakdowns and increasing availability of machines and securing safety of workers. Erring employees were dealt uniformly and procedure was followed to minimize grievances. This consolidated faith in management. Introduction of new incentive scheme was also a step towards recognizing efforts of workmen and staff in production and supply to customers. Efforts were made to conserve financial wealth. Bhuvan felt importance of being a manager of substance. He kept in mind that end result while deciding on issues and also recommended action. It was, therefore, urgent to consider all critical aspects with looked into all facts and information that would aid to decision making. The process of analysis started with asking appropriate questions and examination of related areas and also assessing risks involved. Comparison was made looking into factors; I) likely obstacles in various plants operation, ii) evaluating cost and determining financial resources and iii) human sides before recommending changes. It ensured success and positive results. He demanded results but protected them when they failed and supported them in crises. He spent most of time on shop floor, didn't want anyone to overstay unnecessarily, worked relentlessly to arrange resources, fought for higher incentive and took personal care of employees in distress and visiting ailing employee during hospitalization. In fact he made me omnipresent for his men which made them happy. Once a crane operator misbehaved with one Junior Executive and he took serious disciplinary action to punish operator and didn't bulge despite tremendous pressure from union and seniors. He was criticized but silently appreciated by all for his courage shown. The shop improved and very quickly achieved rated capacity. Foundry was famous for crane operator's problem, where they earned huge hours of overtime in a planned manner. He implemented rotation system in operation of cranes involving heavy duty and light duty cranes and also priority of operation in different bays. Operators were asked to operate all cranes when required. Initially there resistance and he stood near operating cranes to give confidence. This issue settled down with no reduction in production. Secondly he got approved realistic Incentive for employees on target fulfillment basis.

6

Foundry shop faced problem of commissioning of Fluid Sand Process; new production process which was pending for years. It had design deficiency, input was not available. Commissioning in running plant had a repercussion on production. He commissioned system and operated by using indigenous inputs and doubled. In days of final stage of commissioning he ran many times to construction head of zone. He had a peculiar experience when in-charge spending time with women worker during lunch time and disliked interference.

"Why you indulge in immoral acts in work place? You may be booked for causing distress to women employee?"

He replied shamelessly, "I am not alone. This service of one person by many of my colleagues and is known to seniors. We also consume alcohol." He threatened to inform disciplinary authority if work was delayed. He showed no leniency and man became prompt and completed work in time. His confidence in operating production unit enhanced and he expected rise in status and salary both. It happened opposite and was transferred to Administration. He was shocked for few days but accepted it as fate accomplice and never complained. Finally he pulled sell up and started to work to make changes and improve administration. He never cared to hear any loose remark from friends and bosses. Next time he entered new office and started learning new skill. He started meeting officers and staff and worked out strategy. The key word was "Do not fail and Ensure good work." New team became vibrant and Bhuvan felt happy forgetting all that was a past. Sudha became sad for few days but came forward to give personal attention to make conjugal life pleasant.

Big Boss

1

Colonel Gopal came to resort in hill station with wife Disha on invitation from doctor friend Rohit accompanied by wife Sony. He came to enjoy and pass time in games and tracking mainly. Sony was an ease loving woman and believed more in rest and good outside food which were available in resort in plenty. She took dinner just after reaching by car and intended to sleep. Rohit was forced to sleep with her that was second mission for her. She was deprived of intimacy due to engagements of husband covering whole day and many times nights. She was hankering for sex and wanted to satisfy in fifteen days. Colonel kept busy in solving cases as private detective. Difference was that Disha was a sporting woman from college and active with husband. She assisted husband in many ways and showed interest in this work. But she also was not satisfied in conjugal life. Two ladies met often in homes and often talked intimate things. They were popular in social gatherings for their pleasant nature and behavior. One day they discussed about conjugal relation intimately and expressed dissatisfaction in private life.

"Don't you feel that we have become very routine and boring in day to day living?" Sony asked Disha.

"It's natural as men are busy in work and we at home do nothing. We act to ensure a happy family life which is our duty." Disha answered.

"I never thought you to be such dull minded person. Your husband is always boasting about your intelligence and being brave. It all seems to be a blow up to show importance." Sony said satirically.

"You must talk frankly what you want to say," asked Disha.

"I mean we aren't physically satisfied. They come back home tired and go to sleep after dinner. They don't caress or even look faces which keep young and attractive." Sony said opening talk.

"But Colonel entertains me when invited for physical relation. He does with all vigor and full energy. Sometime I fail to adjust with him and he encourages to be active." Disha replied without being shy.

"In my case doctor is exhausted and does all under pressure from me. He is completely mechanical and finishes fast to sleep immediately." Sony replied.

"You are still young and need more of this. I have two grown up children who are in college and going to settle in two years time. I keep busy to organize family. You are free without work and have two maids at home. So you desire more." Disha cleared.

"Do you mean I should start working? I proposed once or twice and Rohit rejected. He thinks I may get trapped in affair with someone and my beauty and attractive figures can allure many. Do I look sexy?" Sony asked.

"Yes you are. Thank god I am a lady otherwise I would have taken you to bed immediately." Disha replied and also laughed.

"Please be serious and suggest from your experience and help. Otherwise I will one day run away from home and you will be responsible for this." Sony opened further.

"Madam, don't talk this shit. I belong to a disciplined family. My father was an army officer and we have been brought under strict vigil," Disha lightly slapped on face of Sony with love.

"You also don't praise army. Many patients come for treatment in clinic of Rohit for sex related disease and some repeat visits. They must have transmitted to their wives. Stories are abundant bosses having relationship with subordinates' wives and maids in houses. Ladies keep busy in kitty parties." Sony became rude.

Disha wanted to avoid discussion any further. She proposed to her.

"Let us go on long vacation to resort in forest where you may seduce your husband for all days. It's about hundred kilometers away. Gopal is member and can get reserved rooms for two couples. You talk to Rohit. We will rest, enjoy food and you do what you desire most." She proposed.

After discussion both agreed to prepare for trip and force husbands to go. Colonel decided to take his car so that doctor couple may remain free. The program materialized and all four travelled to resort in Rangamati. It was a beautiful place with dense forest and nearby and also a big lake. One could swim or take boat for going round lake and place. There was famous temple and deity was renowned for giving blessings which Sony needed to have a child at earliest. They were married for more than ten years and were fit to have child.

2

Setting of resort was very attractive and located off main road about four kilometers. Main road was used for transportation of forest goods by trucks and contractors and forest departments officers visited often to check their working. They had departmental Rest House not very far from resort. Contractors entertained guests with money wine and women; whenever demanded. Call girls and prostitutes came in numbers for different persons and spent night before leaving next day early morning. This helped them to keep privacy. But staffs gossiped about them and made it public. Parties were organized and many times Resort guests joined celebrations for enjoyment.

In was one such party Colonel and Dr Rohit were invited during their stay with wives. They already had spent three days and couples were sounding happy. Their privacy remained intact and Sony often became chirpy and thanked Disha for making arrangements. Gopal smiled and Rohit got embarrassed with open talks and behavior of wife. In friendly gesture they stayed happy.

The chief guest in that party was junior minister who was holding portfolio of forest in state government. He invited guests from other places and wanted them to be entertained. A famous singer and dancer were present to give performance. Drinks flowed and all were drenched in alcohol.

"Now let us disperse to take rest. It's quite late and we may talk in morning." Minister announced and signaled officer to send dancer to his suite.

Gopal and Rohit came back to resort and went into their rooms. They wished each other good night. Sony took many pegs of whisky and was carried by Rohit physically. Normally she was not allowed but here she was given freedom to have drinks and she took without restriction. It was early morning when door of Gopal was knocked by man from reception. Inspector of local police was standing on door.

"What happened officer? Early morning you are here. Anything wrong that has happened." Gopal asked."Sir, please get ready and come with me to Rest House. IG and other senior police officers are on their way to this place. Minister has been killed in night." Inspector spoke with fear in his tone. I am definite to lose my job," he said in nervous tone.

"Give me time to freshen up and I will accompany you in half an hour," replied Colonel and told Inspector to wait at reception.

Disha got up in mean time and was ready to go with Colonel fast while he was talking to Inspector. Her sixth sense worked and she knew her role. This was a system which couple developed together. She took her gun as Colonel avoided to carry any arm. She failed to convince him for doing so. Colonel was a black belt holder and knew other martial arts after being trained by Japanese and Chinese trainers.

Two were present before Inspector. Colonel wrote a slip for doctor so that he was not worried. They reached in short time guest house which was surrounded by police all around. Colonel and Disha looked around and started talking to man who first noticed minister dead in his room.

"Kalim when did you enter room of minister in morning?"

"I was instructed beforehand that minister liked to have tea at five in morning. I entered outer room and kept tea on table and knocked on closed door. Getting no response I pushed door which was open. I had suspicion and further opened to find body of minister in pool of blood. He was lying on bed face down and blood came out from back of head." Kalim was shaking with fear as if he committed crime.

"Don't panic. Nothing will happen to you. Did you touch body by chance?' asked Disha.

"No, I rushed out to inform supervisor who was still sleeping in his room on backside of rest House. One woman got up and fled into forest. This supervisor is habituated and every time after drinking in parties he calls girl from village to sleep. He is a characterless fellow and renowned for this in village. He pays money to keep them silent." Kalim abused supervisor in filthy language.

"What about you? You must also be indulging in this along with supervisor," asked Colonel.

"Yesterday night I was doubly alert as minster was there. I didn't leave my place and sat some distance away from room. I could also watch if someone tried to enter or anyone left." Kalim replied confidently.

"Does it mean you killed minister? Otherwise you must have seen murderer entering or leaving room." Disha spoke in high tone.

"Madam, I don't tell lies. Murderer might have entered and left place when I went for releasing pressure in open in nearby forest. But I returned in ten minutes," Kalim said emphatically.

"Do you have watch to note time so accurately?" Colonel asked.

"No, I estimated time as usual. Of course I also drank with supervisor before his girl came to sleep in room. This happened when minister went to take rest and before girl went into room of supervisor." Kalim replied further.

"Do you know the girl or woman who came to supervisor in night?" asked Colonel.

"No sir, I was already drunk and unstable. Supervisor forced me to take more drink." Kalim replied.

Colonel ordered Kalim not to go away from rest house and asked Inspector to detain him in office of Rest House. They called supervisor who was missing since morning. Other staffs were asked to look for him. After search for a few hours one came running to inform that dead body of supervisor was lying in a bush in forest. It appeared that some animal ate parts of his body.

Inspector went to the spot and saw body and brought in police jeep. Both Colonel and Disha looked at and found one ring in pocket of man. They took it out carefully and kept with them wrapping in handkerchief. Body was sent for post mortem to Government Hospital. Both returned back to Resort and ordered room service fresh tea and breakfast. They discussed details and couldn't conclude anything. Doctor Rohit and Sony were came in their rooms.

"What was the problem that you two rushed to rest House?" asked two together.

"Minister has been killed yesterday night while sleeping. Supervisor of rest house was found dead in forest; part of his body was eaten by some forest animal. Body has been taken by police for post mortem." Colonel briefly told them about incident.

"Colonel, I hope we are safe. In just three days time things have started turning bad. I am an unlucky person. I must go back or Rohit may be in trouble." Sony talked in distress.

"Why you think doctor could be in trouble? How this incident is related to you people?" Disha asked.

"She got panicked. Yesterday night dancing girl came late in night to our room. She was having headache and wanted medicine. I gave medicine and then she requested us to allow her to rest in outer room. She left silently early in morning without telling us." Rohit said.

"So she spoiled one night of Sony despite all preparations." Disha joked and Sony gave a vicious look. "She was an idiot. I was drunk and didn't know if Rohit slept with that girl. Rohit was highly appreciating her during dance." Sony said.

"I think still now she is not normal and must take bath. Then we will take breakfast and talk further." Rohit left with wife and cajoled in corridor. One bearer passing by side smiled.

Colonel and Disha just looked at each other and silently ate breakfast. They ordered fresh tea when there was another knock at door. This time it was IG with his team. There was less sitting space and only IG remained and others walked out allowing them to be alone. Nobody was allowed to disturb till called inside. IG took tea and heard all that was understood by Colonel and his wife.

"This minister was of dubious character and supported terrorist privately and made money through smuggling of drugs. There are many agents in locality who operate here. Many of them were active during his election. Later they freely do robbery and loot to get money. They are not allowed to see him in head quarter and asked to meet during tours to this place. Our life becomes difficult during his stay." IG talked freely."Did you get any clue that killed minister?" Persons who came in contact were police and staff of rest house. New person close to him was dancer whom he invited inside room probably to sleep. She also left quickly and came to get medicine here from my doctor friend." Colonel said without hesitation.

3

Colonel in normal life was keeping busy but spent good time with wife. He always expected to have pleasant and peaceful holiday. He now was engaged in investigating killing of minister which was shocking to him. It was killing of a political heavy weight but few officers turned up. News was kept within local police. Administration was kept off to show their dislike for him who was from lower caste. This finally was to go to higher ups and local police wanted to conclude before informing Home Ministry.

Doctor and his wife looked to be involved in crime and their movements were doubtful. Disha thought about game plan of Doctor and worked independently without telling Colonel.

Local police was aligned with criminals became obvious and were only after money. Politicians and call girls were involved. They together made working in area messy. Once Colonel found persons responsible for killing of one businessman's wife and faced serious challenges and also was attacked. Disha now joined investigation fully ignoring role of Doctor."Colonel, we found out a ring from person of minister. I saw similar ring in finger of Sony. Was it a coincidence or it has some importance?" Disha asked.

"In this case every happening has meaning. IG has given background of dead person which is important local politics. I doubt that person was a duplicate and actual man is missing. We must find out this also." Colonel gave a direction to investigation."I will call two to dining hall for tea while you search their room and belongings which may give definite clue," he continued.

Colonel called on intercom when two were ready after taking bath and moved to dining hall for breakfast and cup of tea. Disha stayed back to join later and went into their room to check. Room was in disorder and she smiled thinking about Sony who must have been violent in night. She checked her dresses, wardrobe and bed and could find nothing useful.

While coming out a man in beard blocked door and attempted to hit with steel rod on head. She was alert and bent side ways to avoid attack. Simultaneously she hit him on face and gave a strong blow and finally floored him. She was trained by Colonel and found useful at such moments. A ring fell from his hand which was similar to that they found earlier. She couldn't conclude anything but pushed man inside washroom and locked.

"I hope you have not finished tea and left some for me. Yesterday food was very rich and I was in trouble for whole night." She said with drawn face to show grief.

"But you still look very fresh, how is it possible?" Sony asked.

"It was mercy of Colonel, who allowed me to sleep peacefully unlike doctor who harassed you all night which is obvious from your face," Disha replied.

"You are wrong, I was sick and he gave me medicine to sleep. I don't know what happened after that. Perhaps dancer came to take medicine for headache which doesn't sound true. These people do so much practice for any performance, that they shouldn't fall sick."

"Minister must have bothered much to make her sick." Sony said.

Colonel asked all to disperse and take rest. He was to proceed with investigation as requested by IG. He moved out to go back to rest house with Disha who now fully involved in absence of regular staff. They examined closely both rings and found them similar. He took out magnifying glass from pocket and found the name of manufacturer who happened to be from Bangladesh. Now it became an international issue and he would need permission of central government to contact authorities there.

"In this situation let us concentrate on local happenings. The man is dead and his post mortem report should disclose what really happened." Disha said.

They were received at gate of guest house by same Inspector who was to remain stationed till next order. The body was still lying in room and was not sent to hospital. This surprised them.

"Other ministers are coming to express grief and then body will be sent for postmortem to capital, which is very abnormal as per rules." Inspector informed.

"You will allow us to see dead body." Colonel asked.

"There is no order stopping you. But madam can't go." He said categorically.

"She is my assistant right now helping in this case." Colonel tried to impress.

"Sorry, I can't disobey orders and you have to take permission of IG. Even Superintendant of Police can't allow." Inspector was adamant.

Colonel went alone inside and saw dead body. He was a different man and minister vanished in some way in night. How this happened was a big question? He examined all places and could find no clue and came out of room. He went to hall and pulled up two chairs in one corner to discuss with Disha.

"The body lying in room is not of minister whom we saw yesterday night. It's a different man. How body has changed? Is minister still alive or dead? These are big questions." Colonel told her.

"This can be found out by questioning bearer who was on duty. He has been kept inside guest house and we can talk to him." Disha suggested.

They came out and started searching him. One man informed that he had gone to attend funeral of supervisor who was his relation also. "This is against order of IG." Disha asked.

"He will be back before IG comes back. Inspector knows and he allowed him to go," the cook informed who was present in guest house.

"You work here as cook. You prepared food according to order given by minister."

"Food for VIPs is brought from star hotels thirty kilometer away. It is brought by them and served when required." The man informed.

"Is anyone from hotel available now? We also took food and whole night suffered. There was something wrong in preparation." Colonel told."I can't say and you may not find anyone to complain. The businessman who was supposed to entertain minister has also gone back with all his men. He came from city only for this. He was a new caterer and not the regular one." The man replied.

4

The case became complicated and Colonel and wife decided to take tour of nearby forest. There was report of wild animal eating part of dead body of supervisor who was a local man and of doubtful character. The man attacking Disha was another person involved. Typical order from IG and adamant behavior of Inspector was also abnormal. Above all dead body changed how and by whom. These were questions hovering in mind of two. Doctor and Sony were supposed to be clean but how and why she went to them and allowed to sleep in room in the resort. Why resort people didn't object entry of unknown woman and no record was kept? These facts made case complex and confusing.

In order to divert their mind and also to relax they took a boat and started going around lake but were cautious knowing attack by enemy who was local and unknown to them. They watched forest and surroundings around and saw few wild boars. Authorities didn't appear to be serious. Colonel was now in romantic mood and he started playing with wife like newly married couple. Disha also played understanding habit of Colonel when he was confused but serious. She knew colonel wanted to think a fresh. Suddenly another motorboat appeared from somewhere and came near them. One man in mask driving boat took out assault rifle and aimed at Colonel. Disha saw as he was coming from behind Colonel and she jumped with husband in cold water. Still some bullets were fired while two swam under water. Colonel went near boat and got into behind man who was standing and pulled him down. He held him and made him choke without breath till he was senseless. He removed mask and was surprised to find Inspector. He decided to dump body in lake but left in boat and two got into their boat to get away. In ten minutes there was blast in boat which sank with body of Inspector. They drove to opposite bank and landed totally drenched in water and took a cab on main road to reach Resort.

Next day news flashed in local papers about death of Inspector. One bearer who came to serve dinner in night informed about mishap. They ate and went to sleep early. Hired boat was gathered by agency in morning when informed by them. This happening was not known to doctor and Sony who remained confined to their room. Both found out way to enjoy vacation in resort.

"Doctor and his wife are habitual drinking persons. Lady consumes heavily and more than doctor. We have never seen such guest in resort." One bearer talked to other in corridor.

"There is order from Boss to keep them drunk so they don't help Colonel in any way who can't find details about killing of duplicate of minister in guest house. Minister presently is in room 303 on third floor." Second man replied in low voice.

They were talking in front of Colonel's room when Disha wanted to go for stroll in compound. She immediately returned and told Colonel what she heard."It could be a ploy to divert attention, still we should verify. Connection between resort and guest house is not clear and manger of resort is never seen." Colonel told wife and ordered room service for tea.

Bearer came with tea and Colonel held him from behind after he kept tray. He was also set man and took out gun from dress to aim. Disha acted fast and hit on his hand to drop gun. Colonel hit on backside of his neck to make him senseless for hours. He was pushed inside wardrobe and door was closed keeping gap for fresh air. He removed dress and Colonel dressed as bearer and went out. He warned Disha to be extra cautious as enemy was around. She signaled alright and took out gun to use if required and locked door. They set their signal to open door when Colonel arrived.

Colonel walked confidently to third floor and rang bell in room no.303. Door was opened by a lady and Colonel recognized dancer in party yesterday night. He went to pickup used cups in tray and bent down. A gun was put on head from behind and he saw the lady standing.

"Who sent you here? Minister didn't order tea for hours." She asked.

"Supervisor in kitchen perhaps got order from Boss on mobile." Colonel replied politely.

"Do you know or recognize boss?" She questioned.

"No, how can I? I am only an employee of contractor working here and joined only last week. Previously I worked in city hotel and supervisor hired me from there." Colonel engaged her in talking and diverted attention. She looked around and time was enough for him to overpower the lady. He took away gun and made her senseless by hitting with butt and dragged body to bathroom. He found minister who was shot at close range. Boss perhaps instructed to do so. He quickly searched room and could find no clues. He walked out locking door and could only be opened by master key in reception. He tiptoed to his room and whistled romantic song tune. Disha opened and quickly ushered him in. The bearer was still lying senseless and Colonel redressed him back. Both walked out locking door and went for stroll slightly away from resort.

They returned and went to check up doctor and Sony. They were normal and enjoying an old movie on TV.

"How is movie?" enquired Disha.

"It's old but romantic. I saw this six times in college with my boyfriend who proved to be a dolt of first order. He once tried to kiss me in open which my brother saw and kicked him out permanently." Sony narrated.

"You must have felt bad." Disha asked.

"I don't like fools. I was saved from getting married to him." She smiled.

"Is it true or you are trying to convince doctor to be an honest wife? He might still be coming to you in absence of doctor. I am surprised you to be obedient here." Disha further said.

"I don't give him free time. You have come and disturbed us otherwise we would have been in bed. We don't bother much for food and eat light in room whenever we get time or feel hungry." Sony said.

"It's too much. Take care of your husband." Disha taunted.

"He is younger to Colonel and performans well. This I realized after coming on this trip." Sony became shameless now. Doctor was getting angry.

"Sorry for talking plain." Sony told doctor

"You ladies have talked enough. Now if you permit I want to discuss with doctor. You move to inside room and leave us." Colonel proposed.

"Doctor, do you recognize this ring? This was found in your room. Similar ring was found near dead body in rest house." Colonel questioned.

"No, I don't know about this. May be Sony knows." Doctor answered casually.

"Is your wife having relationship outside marriage as talked now by them?" replied Colonel.

"I have some doubts. A resort bearer discussed you two drinking heavily. But I find both of you normal. Why this rumor has been spread? Is there any enemy of yours here?" Colonel further asked.

"Yes, Sony is friendly to a member of group who indulge in loot and killing of people. She goes out while doctor is in clinic." Disha came with Sony whose hands she tied with scarf.

"What's this Disha? Why have you tied her hands?" Colonel asked.

"She is not as simple as we thought. She has been gang member from college when her boyfriend introduced her to group in night club. They trapped students with weak financial background and exploited them in many ways.

The woman who tried to assault you some time back, is also in gang. The bearer also is gang member." Disha elaborated.

Door opened suddenly and two persons came in with guns in hands and ordered Colonel and Disha to move out from room. Colonel obeyed along with Disha and walked out locking door behind.

Nothing happened thereafter and silence fell in corridor as usual. It surprised once again Colonel as none searched for bearers he had locked in rooms.

5

Two went out and opened one car forcibly and drove to rest house. They found many administrative persons assembled and discussing about blast that occurred a few hours back there. The room was still in flames where dead body of minister was lying. This made case mysterious. But district authorities didn't come even after two days.

"Why senior officers have not turned up after this incident?" Colonel talked to wife.

"Who knows better than you? Report has been sent by IG that Colonel Gopal is investigating and none other is required. Final report will be sent after findings are finalized by him." A man standing by their side said.

Disha had seen gun in hand of the man which was aimed at Colonel to damage his backbone. Gun was powerful guessed Disha.

"Disha I think we can send final report from a place where computer with internet connection is available." He talked normal.

"Please follow me and I will take you to a place where you can prepare report conveniently and also send. A vehicle is available. You have nothing to do here as dead body is already burnt and nothing could be known." Same person proposed and also pushed them to vehicle which was having dark glasses on windows. This was an old car but in good condition.

They travelled some distance on road and then inside forest which was dense making it a dark area. It was unknown terrain to both and they kept silent on way. After a journey of around one hour, car stopped in front of a bungalow which looked newly painted. It was well furnished and all luxurious items were there. It must be of a very rich and fashionable person. Staff all around was powerful and strongly built. Even women working were well built bodily as if they underwent body building.

Two were ushered in a big hall where a big table was kept at one end of room with only two chairs. They were made to sit there and wait for the boss. Within a few minutes Doctor and Sony were also brought in and kept standing. Boss came in who was well dressed and looked strong. His right leg was odd and bent as if attacked by polio. He had two automatic guns on two sides in cases. He came and sat in high chair to look taller than others. He talked in husky voice which Colonel tried to recognize.

"Colonel and Disha, you two are welcome. In two days time you have made my four agents immobile and crippled. They have been admitted in hospital and will recover in two months time. This has been certified by your doctor friend. I have special weakness for Sony who was my girlfriend right from high school days. Her parents refused to marry her to me and we compromised by meeting frequently in her home and sometimes outside. I saw your wife there only considered to be a danger to me. She has proved right my thinking about her and has been trained well." Boss talked in soft tone.

"What do you want from us?" Colonel asked.

"I want those two rings in which codes for my locker is scripted which only I can read." Boss told.

"One ring was lost when I fought with your man in lake to save us and you recovered him." Colonel said.

"What about the second one?" Boss repeated question.

"That I dropped in room in scuffle with Sony to capture her. It must be found by Sony if she knew its importance." Disha said.

"I didn't know anything about that ring and was suffering so much with beatings from Disha that I didn't try to find it." Sony replied.

"Then I am sorry to announce that all four of you will remain captive in this house while my men try to recover those rings. You are secured here and will be given all comfort. But never try to run away from here. You may be victim of my dumb and deaf guards or hounds roaming in compound." Boss said and walked away.

Inside bungalow they were free to roam and relax. Sony was nervous and wanted to talk. Disha caught hold of her ears and pulled hard to make her cry. In that noise Colonel signaled doctor to keep distance from him and wife and not to open mouth. He knew that all places must be on hidden camera. He checked and found toilet without any camera. He pulled his wife to toilet and discussed.

"This is only place where we are safe. Tell Doctor and Sony writing on their back with lipstick of white color. They should wait for signal to act which will be with hand or fingers." Colonel said and came out of toilet in underpants to mislead recording.

The two couples occupied rooms separated by some distance. They could be seen if walking to other room. Doctor behaved normal and Sony acted on orders from husband which was a good change. Colonel and wife decided to sleep after dinner not thinking of any action. Their question mark on Doctor became deep like surrounding dense forest.

6

Early morning gun fires started as if it was a war field and very sophisticated arms were being used which fired many rounds simultaneously. Sony got up and wanted to rush to Colonel for safety but was rebuked by husband. She slept close to Doctor who kept fondling her like a baby in lap. He laughed silently and kept caressing till fires stopped. Colonel and Disha heard but ignored knowing nothing could be done. Gun fires stopped early morning before sunrise. Their doors were closed and they waited for someone to unlock. It was around ten when door was opened and they were invited for breakfast and man with husky voice still wearing mask welcomed them as if nothing happened few hours back.

"Our business opponents do firing and take away our materials which are imported and precious. These are brought under orders of ministers. We retaliate to silence them. Six persons have been killed and local police will take further care. After breakfast you all will dropped in Resort where you rest and spend remaining days of holidays." The man spoke with complete authority. Doctor and Colonel looked on each other and doubts diminished.

Two couples travelled in different cars which were without dark windows and they could see around. Nothing unusual was seen as told by masked man. They went to rooms after arrival and locked doors to settle down peacefully. Rooms were cleaned and luggage untouched.

"Madam in room 303 has checked out." Colonel was told by reception. IG came to see her off." "Wasthere any other important happening worth knowing?" Colonel asked again."Two dead bodies were recovered from lake and couldn't be recognized. Police is examining." Clerk said.

Doctor came from back and put hand on Colonel's shoulder. "What are you enquiring about? Yesterday we couldn't sleep and take rest. Our holiday has been spoiled," he said.

"Is it so? This has to be confirmed by Sony." He winked and smiled.

They came back to rooms and Disha called Sony on intercom in evening. Colonel asked her to be in this room with Disha and was going out. He looked unhappy not to find culprit despite being present around. It was frustrating for him and visible on face. He advised them to remain locked after dinner till his return. He analyzed with Disha total incident in mean time.

She said, "It's a mixed case of terrorism, administration failure and business interests. The man with husky voice is the boss. Minister was asked to go leaving next man who was adversary of boss and got eliminated. The lady in room 303 killed so called minister who came to sleep with her. IG is renowned corrupt person as told by guest house staff previous day when we went to see dead body and was prevented. IG wanted us to be killed and help woman in all acts. He sent hired killer as Inspector to do this."

"I can't say right now before gathering more details. I must check Resort and Guest house records. I have set two persons to give relevant information." Colonel talked firmly.

Doctor and his wife were in their room. Sony brought gun which was lying under bed placed carelessly and likely to be picked up later. She also found ring lying inside drawer of bed at far end. These all showed that a visitor entered room in their absence. It was also not clear why the cleaning man didn't move these from room. Both were highly disturbed and felt danger on lives. But they didn't tell Colonel about apprehensions.

"Colonel, come to my room. I have to discuss some urgent problems. Sony is here." Doctor talked over intercom. Colonel came to room of doctor leaving Disha. He asked doctor to order tea. All sat down and he heard him who gave all detail and his views. Doctor was in terror and Sony unnerved and stayed unmoved. She packed up to leave the place early in evening.

"It appears you are going back leaving us alone to rejoice beautiful surroundings, lake and comfort of resort," questioned Colonel.

"Only you can enjoy this place after seeing all what happened yesterday and day before. You have nerve of steel and your wife has heart made of reinforced materials. I have been shaking since I returned to this room and found gun and inauspicious ring," replied Sony in tears.

"You forgot to mention that three days back you were constantly playing in lap of doctor and felt being in heaven which you desired. Are you happy now? Doctor won't be looking at you after getting back to work and starts counting notes to stuff in bag to make you happy," Colonel smiled viciously.

"I never thought you can also talk like this. Disha can only bear your assault and I am lucky to have softer doctor with me," Sony made face and said. She was angry with Disha who told all private talks to him. Colonel must be a Romeo in college days and trapped charming woman, Disha. Colonel stopped and told two about the plan of action now. He asked them to stay and go back together otherwise neighbor may doubt our broken friendship.

Colonel came back after taking tea and asked Sony to come along to his room. Two ladies locked themselves inside after taking dinner in room only. They quarreled for some time for discloser of intimate talks to husbands. It was difficult to sleep under tension. According to Colonel all was to happen that night only.

Colonel walked outside in open when resort manager walked from back side quarters He checked detail from Desk clerk and moved towards rooms for inspection of dining hall where he sat down to have drink and food. His intention was to kill some time. Colonel also walked in and went to room of doctor who was awake and reading cine magazine. He got inside wash room hiding after giving instructions, who gradually felt more terrified.

Door bell rang and doctor opened to receive Resort manager and made him sit. They exchanged curtsies lightly and shared experiences in this place.

"I have come to collect two things from this room. In your absence yesterday night my wife left a gun and her diamond ring in this room. She drank too much and was unfit to go home. She slept here after my permission. I am sorry for this which was against rules of Resort." Manager was extremely polite.

"I didn't find any gun or ring what you are telling. You may check yourself." Doctor told.

"Your wife must be sleeping in bed." He asked.

"She has not returned from friend's room and talking long which is her liking and enjoys. We have come here together." Doctor clarified.

"Gun is not here. Even ring is missing from drawer where wife kept. You are a liar doctor and you have to pay for this with your life." Manger pulled out gun from his pocket and aimed at him.

"No it won't be so Raghav. You drop your gun." Colonel walked out from washroom and held his hand firmly. He snatched gun and kept in his pocket.

"Colonel, you are still here. I was told you have already left this place." Manager said.

"You faked IG in all your acts before us. Real man must be coming any moment and you will give statement to police. I am only a guest here." Colonel concluded.

Manager tried to jump on Colonel as expected and he moved side allowing him to drop on floor and hit knee with boot to make him immobile. IG and other police officials came inside and arrested him. Two guns and diamond rings were given to police. They thanked Colonel and went out. Next morning four assembled on breakfast table and Colonel explained.

"I doubted when we were released from captivity without any harm and kept respectfully. Manager and his wife wanted to cool down in our rooms after incident of Guest House to misguide police. I saw defective left leg of Big Boss often talked on different occasions. This I noticed when he posed as IG in Rest House on day of incidence and finally today in lobby. I understood his move after his wife left and now caught him easily. IG was informed beforehand who came to arrest him."

"How you are identifying culprit so easily?" asked Sony.

"Just as you trap Doctor with your beauty and have pleasant nights. You had so last night and marks are on your face," Colonel replied.

"You can't tease my friend like this," Disha looked sternly at husband.

Deity Arrives

1

Puja was over and so noise which disturbed life round the clock closed. It was madness in a way when children and youngsters got engaged in celebration of Goddess of Learning. It's faith which has been since many years. Question comes who started this and why. One school of thought considers it as fictitious existence created by imaginative scholars to discipline society in matters of learning. He described convincingly which was further knitted into tale in epics where millions of such gods and goddesses appeared and made story interesting. Idea also was to keep human mind engaged after limited period working in agricultural activities. Free time was bound to disturb social order and many indulged in unwanted activities upsetting law and order. Fear of god and their curses threatened to punish for wrong doings. Less thinking and with less analytical minds accepted whatever was said by scholarly pundits. These pundits explained verses written in Sanskrit and elaborated in simpler words for masses to understand which also included warnings of ill fate and sufferings if not followed in true sense in daily life. Innocent people thought only to ward off natural calamities and save life someway. This was an easier way chanting some prayer and offering eatables to deities and get blessings for peace and existence. People never knew how it happened and any abnormal changes or happenings was assumed to be anger of god who lived somewhere in heaven. This type of understanding travelled all those days till scientific revelations didn't happen. Study of science made people thinking and interpreting differently all that happened. They understood laws and forces operating in nature and how those could be controlled. Natural mishaps were sudden and severe which shook people within. They worked to rebuild and nature disrupted which was more painful and complete belief on science couldn't happen. Stories of epics were more interesting and all heard them time and again from saints and scholars. These were easier to comprehend being closer to life and faith in deity and worships continued round the year.

One reason for this was festivity which gave relaxation and indulgence in spending for new dresses, ornaments and also in many societies picking up life partners. These occasions also brought cases of exploitations to fore and wrong deeds got exposed. Society punished them in own way but law and order became tighter and also exploitative. Politics entered into celebrations and started developing as vote banks. Caste struggles and group fights increased and uncertainties also grew in numbers. Again blind faith was back in operation and even educated depended on these. It gave doubt whether we are developing or returning back to old ways. Criminals made this more painful and threatened moneyed people for extortion. All succumbed and responded by hired gunmen for whom money making became easier and at times traumatic.

Law was unable to stop and faith in god and deity worshipping was back in different forms. Number of participants increased and many long processions could be seen. Life of general mass was put into difficulties upsetting working and discipline. Police confused mostly and remained just observers and to act when big disorder happened. All said, "God you are great and save us from perils".

Kanu lived in a settlement near town. This started with few huts and gradually men and women from villages came to stay and work in homes of people wanting helping hands. Wealthy women in town stopped doing menial work and after sometime cooking too. Their men were forced to eat food prepared by these uneducated and dirty men and women who generally didn't know hygienic living habits. Life continued and poor people kept earning. Their exploitations also came to light which were never fought and absorbed for staying in job.

All well to do popped up tablets and medicines in larger quantities and expenses on doctors increased. Their numbers also increased and whole population queued for treatment starting early morning. Deprived people wanted more money and all bad practices developed including thefts, loots and snatching in streets. Mafia and antisocial became active and their groups became more aggressive. Police had to work overtime and many of them connived with disturbing forces for self gain. Everywhere politics entered and daily life became more torturous. Kanu fell once in such association. His mother was widowed and married another man in settlement; who was a small contractor. He had children from first wife who lived in village. Sadhu was not as name suggested. He was a drunkard and a womanizer. Kanu's mother tolerated for safety of son and self and was not strict about morality. Kanu followed mother and her values in life since childhood. He learnt to become self reliant and started selling coke on cycle at ten o'clock only. He carried ten bags of coke on cycle and walked distance of ten kilometers to market. On way also he sold bags if there was any buyer. This way he earned almost two hundred rupees a day which he deposited in bank and maintained a joint account with mother. His mother learnt signing name with son when he started going to free school run by one NGO. Both mother and son ate dinner together as a rule when Kanu took bath and sat in front with separate steel plates given by house mistress where mother worked. Their faces gradually radiated with filled up belly. Mother slept only after Kanu. Son knew from noise made by drunken father when he visited late night and behaved like angry animal. Kanu prayed silently for safety of mother and her well being. Father never gave money and on reverse took money from mother before leaving in morning when Kanu was already out on his job of gathering coke bags. He could never account for how much money was taken but never stopped mother from giving. It was a peculiar relationship.

"Why don't you kick father out from hut who tortures you?" Kanu asked.

"I can't do that. He is my husband and like God. He has saved me in difficult days and I pay him back with pleasure he wants in being together." Mother replied.

"Your God is not good and always gives pain. Why don't you forget him?" Kanu questioned next.

"No he is great and has gifted you. You will take care of me when I am facing problem in old age and you must grow big." Mother said and moaned.

"Not me but money I am collecting in bank. It will be spent when you fall sick and become weak. But now you mustn't ignore health. I know you don't eat whole day because I keep without food." Son replied differently.

"That is true. You are working harder than me. I eat in house of mistress who gives me remains daily. They waste food because often master comes after eating outside. She quarrels as her man spends time with other women just like your father. Males have this freedom." Mother spoke without hesitation.

Kanu never heard complete story as he slept fast being dead tired after day's work. Mother smiled and patted son on cheek and prayed god for his safety and well being. God was a strong link between two and never vanished. This was life of poor and all dwellers were having similar stories. Morning started again with same routine. He took break on Mondays when he worshipped in Shiva Temple in nearby colony directed by mother. He took early bath and changed in fresh clothes and walked with water mixed with milk in a pot and flowers in it. He prayed for long almost half an hour. Nobody could say what prayer he recited. One could see rolling tears from his eyes after ten minutes which continued for next fifteen to twenty minutes. Mother prepared breakfast before going to work who had no break. She never took break not to lose daily brunch and tea. Often she sat in front of landlady and sipped tea for long fifteen minutes. Landlady shared her painful stories about bad behavior of husband and wanted blessing from God for peace and harmony in conjugal life.

"Why Kanu doesn't work on Mondays?" She asked.

"He believes in Shiva the almighty and believes him to be responsible for creation and destruction of world. He heard in one congregation in town where he went to collect money from regular customer, who happened to be a woman. Thereafter he decided to please Shiva worshipping on Mondays. He asks me to accompany but I can't. I have to work here not to disturb your routine." Kajal said.

"What he does after worshipping in temple?" lady asked further.

"He comes back and sleeps for few hours. Later he goes with friends to market and eats some food of choice. He comes back by the time I am at home. He takes lunch with me and sleeps again till evening." Kajal replied.

"Why you allow him to go to market? He will get spoiled." Lady expressed concern.

"No he won't as he is Shiva worshipper who guides him." Kajal clarified.

"How is it possible? You ask him to see me next Monday. I want to talk to him." Lady instructed.

Next Monday Kanu went to house of land lady after breakfast. His mother was working. He sat on ground in front and was impressed by her personality. She quarried about Shiva.

"You look like Durga, wife of Shiva. Your face glows like and you can't harm anyone. Now I understand why mother is so strong. She gets strength from you and bears tortures of life happily. Father gives her pains when he visits home fully drunk and behaves like wild animal."

Mother came running and shouted, "Don't talk ill of father. He is also like your Shiva and you are fruit offered to me." He looked at mother and expressed sorrow by touching her feet. Mother became happy and went back to work. Landlady couldn't understand and she called Kanu's mother to give food kept especially for him.

"This is after I have worshipped Shiva in morning before you came. You take this and give me blessings." Landlady asked.

Kanu failed to understand but ate with interest the sweet dish. He finished and told, "It was very tasty. I never ate such good preparation. Shiva will certainly fulfill you desire."

Kanu got up and ran to temple and prayed second time on that day. This time he prayed loudly.

"Lord Shiva you must bless landlady with a son. She is in great sorrow in absence of child. You direct her husband to behave well with her. She believes me because I have great faith in you. You must not fail my faith."

He came back to find mother at home. "Where have you been? I am waiting for you since last one hour. Landlady has given these clothes for you which she bought last evening from market. She is very good woman."

Kanu said, "I went to pray for her. She was looking very sad. I have asked Shiva to bless with son which will make her happy."

She was asking me other day to give you to him. I refused as I can't survive without you.

"I knew this from her look. That's why I went to Shiva to pray for child. I also can't leave you."

It happened so and landlady got pregnant after few months and mother informed about this. Kanu never went to her place despite several requests conveyed by mother. No amount of persuasion could change his decision. He concentrated on work. Of late police demand for money increased and his income reduced substantially. Kanu discussed with mother and sought opinion for new job. Mother from experience suggested him to enter into trading of goats which was always high in demand. He visited village and bought many goats and sold at high profit. It increased substantially during festivals when goats were sacrificed before deity by many and meat was consumed by community. Deity became important for Kanu.

Mother decided to get Kanu married at an early age which was not considered bad. Bride was of small but became mother without problem. This was celebrated by family and relatives. Kanu was not happy and he took great pains to take care of child. Very quickly child gained health and became strong after taking rice juice and very coarse grains. His wife Kumud also started working in houses part time and child care was done by other family members turn by turn. There was good understanding which allowed all to survive in happiness and sad moments.

"Now I want my son to read and write. I will be given all support and facility." Kanu declared. He didn't select free school where child progressed very slow and left reading after few years of schooling. He increased his earning and asked son to do well. In few years result was visible and Sonu went to high school and successfully completed course. Then he went to college to obtain degree and stayed in hostel. He visited home during leave and concentrated on studies. Kajal took good care as directed by husband. All started living in harmony.

During one holiday Kanu decided to worship Goddess of Knowledge, Saraswati. This was performed for one day only and deity was placed on pedestal at place of worship. Place was decorated and chanting of verses by priest was done. Thereafter cultural program was conducted by groups till late in night. Kanu spent whole night with deity and continued to protect till submersion in river next day. He ate only vegetarian food with all family members, different from other festivals. He developed faith that worship brought good results in examination. Finally Sonu got very respectable job and started earning.

"How are you feeling now?" Kanu asked wife. Kajal didn't reply.

"I am very happy and will try to fulfill your aspirations. I must also remember blessings of deity who told me every time to remember good work and humanity while performing duty." Sonu replied instead of Kajal.

"When did you talk to deity?" Kanu wanted to know.

"During worship in night hours when all slept."

"I didn't hear a word. How you could listen?" Kanu quarried.

"It was through realization within self. It was consciousness which worked. My education has given this to me. I am grateful to you father." He bowed on feet of father. Kajal blessed along with Kanu.

Kanu was serious and emotional. He grabbed son close and started shedding tears. He felt deity arrived when son completed study and got into respectable position in society. Kajal kept looking at both and shared her own feelings.

Next time goddess was worshipped with greater enthusiasm and whole community was inspired by success of Sonu. Music and dance was performed by kids and youngsters whole night. Next day again it was whole community bidding farewell to goddess. Many women gave tearful adieu. All prayed goddess to stay in heart and inspire children to study and get success. This could only ensure better life for families. Kanu stood in front guiding movements while his wife was in big crowd with her head raised high.

Kuruvilla Home

Rose Kuruvilla was travelling South of Mandak which was a dense forest area where darkness prevailed even in day time. Tribes in area were illiterate and knew nothing about civilized society. People lived mainly on forest produce and cultivated small pieces of land to grow rough grains which were also consumed by animals. They thrived mainly on berries and roots available since years. People in area were semi attired and elderly ladies and gents were walking around topless. Their customs were peculiar and selection of bridegroom was done on counts of wild animals killed in their past years right from childhood. Girls liked to compete with boys willing to marry and chased same wild animal in jungle. If boy was able to kill animal first he could propose to girl right on spot and got married near the forest deity which was just some vaguely shaped stone marked with vermillion. These Gods or Goddesses were worshipped by offering forest birds. They all believed strongly and offered fresh blood of kills and also sipped raw to get strength. Ordinarily outsiders couldn't see sight and anyone uttering unwanted word or insulting traditions were surrendered to Village Chief who punished them to work as slave to village for some period. In case village chief was convinced by innocence of any punished man he was freed early and respectfully transferred out of forest with total protection.

Rival groups tried to recapture such victims to make them captive, which was treated insult of chief. They fought with each other for long in hide and seek manner till a compromise through missionary was reached.

Women were given concessions in all activities and even in competition as mark of respect for becoming mother. They were never given harsh treatment and were made to serve long elderly women in person. They conducted job of child birth like nurse and were helped by seniors. This was training and learning time for them. Sick ladies were not allowed to go outside in forest for nature calls or collecting food and were fed by these serving women. At times their life was made difficult if they made mistakes which resulted in death of newly born child up to age of five. Thereafter boy or girl became member of hunting groups with elders and learnt to gather food and also kill birds and rabbits for food. They were taught making fire and cooking in earthen pots which were fragile and often gave way on fire with slightest mistake. This skillful job was test for readiness for marriage and it was not hurried. Most girls lost virginity at an early age and none mind this. Village chief certified their preparedness to society when they were invited to run race or compete. If girls won in hunting they were given preference to select boy of their choice. She was allowed to break marriage with early pronouncement and expression of desire. She was asked to run to their home some distance away and husband was asked to chase to stop. In case she reached before being caught, she was free to marry again.

In many tribes there was system of demand and supply of numbers of chicken as dowry which were used later in feast after marriage. It was also accompanied with bottles of local drinks prepared from rice at home. The superior variety was made from Mahua fruits and given in limited numbers served to respected men and women attending functions. The total life of these tribal was knitted in such a fashion that confused for years if he tried to understand. Traditions varied widely at short distance within forest and it prevailed in all areas in forest. They suffer throughout life and die in harness most times.

Rose Kuruvilla was born from a tribal mother and a Christian father who served church and fathers residing in there. Kuruvilla was born in missionary hospital and studied in school and college run by them. She was a brilliant girl and good in study. She was also a good in sports and won medals and trophies. Her father expected her to study and become an officer in government. She started preparing and was through in all competitive examinations. She got good rank in selection and was sent for training to government training center. Her first posting was in tribal area which changed her mind after seeing plight of people residing in these villages. After many years of development they remained ill educated and with bad habits. They didn't change their belief despite efforts from Christian Institutions. Although they gained economically and started using common dresses and practiced healthy life style. They kept well and clean and were more hygiene conscious then general people.

Rose engrossed in thinking about life of tribal and took journey to go into deep forest on weekends. She tried to return back next day by evening. She bought a second hand government jeep in auction and got it converted making arrangements in back side to sleep two persons. This was convertible in day time and worked as kitchen. She carried ration, adequate water and a kerosene stove. Often she purchased vegetables on her way before entering into forest. In short she arranged everything for two days camping. One another person accompanied her who was also studied life of tribal. He worked on research project from university where he worked and published papers in international journal which got high appreciation. Two carried one portable type writer which was used for recording experiences and stories while camping. It was done in light of kerosene lamp, another essential for spending nights in forest. They maintained strictly distance while sleeping in congested space of vehicle.

Generally they camped inside village among houses of tribal which was filled with smoke of burning flesh. Village people used to party in evening and ate together animal they killed in hunting which were cooked on flame of pier being burnt. Country liquor was available in plenty made from rice in earthen pitcher. Pitcher was filled with rice and water for days and kept in pits under earth for almost a week. This was taken out on party days. Otherwise they ate cooked rice added with salt, red chilies in plenty. Whole family took this mix in large aluminum bowl. One bowl was enough for all after drinking liquor in large quantity and cooked meat. Their capacity was high and many got intoxicated and played games after eating which included men and women both. Unmarried girls and boys were kept away and allowed to observe game to practice after being married. Strictly couples couldn't be differentiated and a mix was possible; which was tolerable to all. In morning they forgot and started their daily routine work. Ladies went to forest to pick up dry woods and leaves. Young girls took care of kitchen and collecting water from nearest brook or pond. This type of life was very attractive once watched closely. One may get submerged and totally lost. Of course some fall prey to wild animals and seriously injured and finally found dead not getting medical aids.

It happened in one such trip with Rose and her friend. She was camping inside village and ready with dinner in night. Her friend was typing his observations. Two three men and women knocked on door of jeep and forced them to come out. Both were invited to night party. That day party was served with chicken and liquor from jungle berries; which was superior in taste. They were offered first drink which both relished and took in large quantity. They liked half cooked chicken on wooden fire and tasted different. Both returned to jeep fully intoxicated and fell into jeep somehow locking on door from inside. Beds were opened and both slept till late in morning to find laughing group of young boys and girls. They soon realized themselves to be half dressed and looked at each other in suspicion but kept mum. They took time to normalize and started their day as usual. It was second day and they roamed around to study vegetation and fields developed by locals to grow grains and vegetables mainly roots which could be cooked for eating. They were back to jeep and cooked lunch of rice and vegetables and ate in large quantity feeling hungry. Both were happy that last night food didn't upset their stomach. Suddenly Rose wanted to stay one day more to enjoy party in night. Her friend was hesitant as he was to miss his classes. He finally agreed on terms not to join party in night.

Fire was lighted and drum beatings started. Group songs were being sung and it was party of young boys and girls. Two girls came and pulled Rose out to sing and dance with them. She couldn't resist and went ahead. Her friend stayed back and later went out to see dancing. Rose was totally engrossed as if she was one of them. One very young fellow was dancing constantly with her and they embraced each other. Perhaps she was drunk. Party was over and she didn't eat anything and slept. Next morning was scheduled for departure and she found self to be lazy.

'Yesterday you danced long with that young boy. You liked his company.'

'Same as I liked your company yesterday night inside jeep.'

'We must go back today.'

'No I am staying back. You go with jeep and come back next week end with enough ration for a month with fuel and other materials. I want to spend some days with these people and understand their needs. I want to devote life in their service.'

'It's a brave decision. How will you stay alone?'

'That young boy has agreed to serve me and protect me.'

'He is too young for you to marry.'

'Who told you I am marrying him. He is just like son and I shall take care of him like mother. He is an orphan and needs care.'

'This again is very brave posture. How are you going to spend time here?'

'Let time pass and we will know. But you must come with jeep and materials next week end. Also bring motorcycle so that you may go back. Bring cycle in jeep which will be used by this boy while working here. I will need his services in several ways.'

Finally her friend Mohit returned back alone and looked sad. He fell in love with Rose and next day it was highly dejected. Once he thought to force her to come along. But he knew the determined woman in her which could revolt strongly. He didn't get chance even to share feelings and express what he wanted. Rose understood but decided to keep away for doing what she felt necessary in last two days. It was not new as in earlier visits to this forest area attracted her to serve and improve life of poor suffering in loneliness of forest. She could not describe how moved she got within. Now she wanted to test all her thinking as ground realities.

Mohit came back with all that was told next week end. He found a hut was standing made of wood and leaves strong enough to keep away wild animals in middle of village. He stayed for few hours and left on motorbike praying for her safety. He couldn't realize a lie could take turn so fast for unknown reasons and objectives. No parting words were uttered and he was waved with faint smile on lips which he sucked last night feverously and felt satisfied. He still reflected on sweetness and different taste never experienced earlier in any other girl he slept with consent and for days. Dreams in mind of Rose stayed permanently on his lips and words too.

Next day she took permission from guardian of Soma to stay with her in hut. Her behavior impressed all uneducated villagers. This was finally confirmed when Father Robert from City church visited. He came twice a month to check these people for years living and gave them assistance of clothes, food, medicines and books for children who attended his classes for half day. He also preached verses from Bible and stories from religious books in simple language.

He learnt local dialect and mostly talked in their tongue. All waited for his visits and served him simple food which he ate without reservation. He also took drink from them to prove their love and affection. Rose was surprised but attended those meetings. Father Robert knew about Rose being educated and all was told to him by Mohit to ensure safety in his absence. Father wanted her to join church and receive assistance in her work and she refused. She kept her faith and everyday prayed before framed painting of Krishna for half an hour. She believed Krishna came to this world before Christ to change life of people in different way which was based on action, music and group dance. He promoted free mixing of men and women through cultural activities and suggested open mindedness for betterment of society and people. He became God incarnation in years to follow. "Father I want to work with them and carry on your mission if you allow.'

'How can you do that as this program is decided by church authority? I can't allow you without taking permission from them.'

'Please take permission and I shall work. You shouldn't object if otherwise also I work for improvement in their living condition and other life related matters.'

'Of course you continue and none can stop you from rendering services to humanity. But any financial needs won't be available to you from us.'

Rose kept silent and Father Robert left by his motor bike on which he used to travel. He looked like tourist and mingled with population on his way. He stopped in several places to learn needs of people and provided help. His mission also was to spread religion. Rose understood but she had no intention to oppose. She now concentrated on own work and started changing life in village.

She first started teaching Soma and trained him as driver. He was intelligent and a fast learner and within months he could read and write. He drove jeep to market near railway station four kilometers away. He drove on forest roads and stopped by side whenever Lorries came his way. KURUVILLA was painted on front and hood which became symbol for quick. Forest contractors recognized efforts of Rose and gave fuel to vehicle from their pumps or storage in large drums whenever required. Many of them visited Rose while travelling inside forest or returning back. Rose served them tea and biscuits. In turn they donated money for small clinic constructed and run in village. They helped to find a doctor in town who visited once a week free of charges and brought free medicines. Villagers generally relied on jungle medicines not known to outsiders. Rose collected information and started preparing them with help of seniors who knew the method of preparation. This served in measure quantity and least objected by local population. Rose was being called doctor Didi.

One school building with three rooms and a large verandah was made with money and manpower to assist Rose in teaching work. This news spread in jungle and children from nearby clusters started attending classes. Rose also offered them services of jeep to ferry them to station and marketing in weekly bazaar when she went with Soma. She was respected by people selling goods in market and offered rebates without asking. Soma became expert and often pressed for rebates as he served food to many needy persons. All were asked to work in construction of KURUVILLA HOME which they took up by side of present residence of Rose. Shortly she was given name of Madam Didi or madam in short, which became famous inside forest. Her life changed and she forgot her past. She felt it to be a new birth amongst forest residing population. But she maintained her dignity and respect and often was seen to be strict with defaulters.

Madam went once or twice a week to post office in market near station to drop letters and also talk over phone to known people. All those acquainted started sending donations to and she collected fund which was kept inside home. The wooden home was double storied made with wood supplied by forest contractors from depot after cutting and shaping. They also engaged paid carpenters. The building was painted all green by Soma and his friends. Lily was young girl attracted to Soma from childhood and finally got married in community celebration. Now three persons resided in Home. Madam was having free time when young pair did all work and worked with full responsibility.

Rose found time to write experiences in diary every day for two hours. She recorded all that happened and praised Soma and Lily for all work done. The village changed and children started going to schools in town by train on monthly passes got made by Madam. Jeep dropped them in time and received at station in afternoon. Their home work was checked by her in evening and given further lessons. Villagers were sent for training in crafts and many got job in town with help of Madam, who visited them in work places to ensure their satisfactory performance of job. Woman also changed their ways of working and formed groups to do hand crafts from dried forest woods which became fashion.

A few were sent in exhibitions and got rewarded. These items were named Kuruvilla Crafts.

Reputation spread and visitors from far and distance started visiting Kuruvilla Home and picked up items of liking round the year. Names of awardees appeared in news papers which were preserved carefully. All these were recorded by her in diary which ran in volumes in years which passed.

'Madam someone wants to see you?' Soma told her.

'Make him sit in outside room. I am coming after finishing my diary for the day.'

She came out to find Mohit waiting to see her. He had grown old but Rose looked less old and more attractive. He couldn't believe his eyes.

'I think your sincerity in work has put glow in your face. I can see changes brought in village. I was given a complaint against you by church authorities about misuse of funds given to you. I am District Development Commissioner and asked to enquire.'

'No fund has been given by church. All donations have come from people and forest contractors. We have not cut a single tree from forest and planted trees in vacant areas by taking saplings from forest department. You can verify from them. I have kept all accounts which you can check and satisfy.'

All records were given for checking by DDC and lunch was served by Soma and Lily who introduced themselves as volunteers of Kuruvilla Home. Mohit ate food and got ready to go. Soma offered to drop him to station in jeep which was kept in good order.

'You should have come by own vehicle.'

'I left my car some distance away not to alert you all about my coming. I am satisfied with all detail and now walk down to my car on foot. I don't want any obligation from your home.'

Mohit walked back to his car again very sad for the work he was given to do doubting sincerity of woman who gave life for these development works without assistance from government or any agency. He turned and saluted Kuruvilla Home and got lost fast in forest.

Rose Kuruvilla worked all time for village to change their lives and results started coming. One boy became state champion in arrow shooting in state and was being trained for national meet. Two girls won medals in track events and were also selected for national championship meet. Two women became instructors in trade center in town and made silk dresses.

Those in villages got engaged in developing plots for crops and vegetables and fruit farming. These fruits were sent to town in juice making factory and were seeking brand name. All these were getting support from people working outside. Kuruvilla now travelled minimum and all was left to Soma who was well trained. Lily was constantly in service of madam who was all time engaged in recording of developmental activities. A day came when Kuruvilla was nominated for coveted recognition at national level and village celebrated occasion for full one week. Nobody could imagine the level of performance which was mainly done in day time. Only parties were held around fireworks and all were allowed to have food and drink to their satisfaction. Proud Kuruvilla watched gracefully from her home which was decorated well and lamps glittered around. She continued her work and Kuruvilla Home became important destinations for tourists to understand work of a devoted woman after sacrificing all pleasures of life. She could have better life with education in her hand but preferred to work for betterment of tribal living away from modern society. She fell sick one day and even with care of Soma and Lily couldn't survive. Villagers performed last rites in their way and one artist made a state of the lady in front of Kuruvilla Home. They started worshipping her in this form. Her diaries were got printed by Mohit and given to libraries. Now he took charge of the home and continued working more vigorously.

Living in Pain

1

Sanad Kumar, Ashu's grandfather was a school teacher in village high school. He was highly respected for brilliance in mathematics and was a renowned teacher. He taught privately to students to earn in evenings in batches. Each group consisted of twenty five students and came to his residence. This enhanced income and his living was much better compared to other teachers. He was hard working and supported parents financially through his earnings that resided in village and were small farmer. Ashu's mother Rima was a Bengali girl and daughter of a railway official posted locally. Rima also started taking tuition from Sanad in evenings and was not very regular. She came in any of batch and for this Sanad banged her severely one day when she started crying before students.

"Why are you crying? What is your problem in coming in the defined batch?" asked Sanad.

She kept crying and finally he closed class early. Rima didn't leave the place and kept standing.

"Why don't you go home?" asked Sanad

"I am scared of step mother who will bang if I reach home before scheduled time. This time she is busy with other man who comes regularly to our house. He also looks at me with lust and I am afraid he may spoil me and mother may support to defame me and kick out from home. She warned her earlier several times that if I entered home before time, she will encourage visitor to sleep with me. My father doubts mother, but he can't open his mouth with a fear she may create scene and implicate me with father."

Sanad was confused and couldn't force Rima to go away and she stayed back. Gradually she started coming early in evening and stayed in Sanad's house to spend time rather than take tuition. She also served snacks and tea to him intermittently to impress that she was a good cook. This closeness developed into attraction and one day she went in his bed room and left place after great persuasion. Sanad also developed weakness for girl and one day he married her in local temple without informing parents.

Later Sanad's father knew and got annoyed and broke all relations. One day, after many years on insistence both went to see parents in village and returned from door. This was fresh in mind of Rima which forced her now to accept marriage of Ashu and Nina without much resistance. Later Sanad also reconciled and decided to support grandson. He was happy that Nina was good looking and able to manage house efficiently and supported his wife.

"Cross cultural life settings had their own woos which couple and family members tolerate as many adjustments were required. Main constraint was limited social circle and many didn't entertain these trend setters and always felt it to be against norms. Modernization brought changes, but mental blocks didn't vanish till liberalized norms developed in community. Education facilitated but was still not a cure for such limited approach in any conservative society." Sanad pondered while sipping morning tea and Rima gossiped her favorite topics of social bickering endlessly.

Ranbir was son of a landlord and brought up in a lavish way and was fashionable. He came to study in town and lived in rented house and later purchased it and modified to make it bungalow with many modern amenities. He had enough money to do this. His father came to stay for day or two with son. He was more concerned with his extensive landed properties in village, constantly under threats from communists who became active. Ranbir was influenced by communist movement and started pleading cases of peasants against injustice and atrocities. Exploitation of females of all age groups by landlords was quite prevalent in village. His father also was involved in few cases which created a type of aversion in him for own family. He often told this to mother. Once he saw his elder brother Sudhir indulging in sex with maid inside cow shade. His brother paid paltry sum after ordeal which she refused for fear of getting punished by landlord or own mother. They felt obliged to be engaged in these households for bread, clothes and shelter and some small piece of land which father cultivated to get crops and support family. They considered landlord as god and waited all time to receive orders and follow without any resistance for small favors in daily life.

Ranbir was disturbed and stopped coming home during summer vacation or long breaks from college and visited cities and places for touring and sightseeing. His interest in social activities increased and he became comrade in Communist Party. On getting report father asked him to leave house and mother cried for days. Even his elder brother supported father. It was beneficial for him to become heir of all properties. Father had already given one house in town where he lived. Also enough money was given to peruse studies. Mother wanted to give him more which was refused. They knew that money would be transferred to Communist Party. Father told her, "Look he may donate all money to party as trend is prevailing now in youngsters joining the cadre of Communists. Government is also taking action against them. They indulge in subversive activities. You shouldn't be surprised if one day he is sent to jail."

"Oh God; what has gone wrong with this boy and why are we getting punished for no fault of ours? It must be curse of your misdeeds and exploitation in village you indulge frequently. Sudhir is on your path only. He always thrashes wife for small reasons. He brought a girl other day in bedroom at dead of night which wife objected and was beaten," complained mother.

"Don't talk rubbish? This is our right as landlords and we can enjoy any woman of choice whose family is dependent on us. You be confined in home and produce children, which is a pious duty. Get reasonable comfort and don't challenge us. You better get lost and look after household and let me know if anything is required by family." Sanad replied angrily.

She started sobbing and felt like ending life in some way, but immediately remembered younger son who was yet to settle in life. One thing became certain that she stopped sharing bed with husband. She slept independently in inside room locked firmly. This was minimum punishment she could give and never got pregnant again. Her husband once in anger charged her being cold impotency which she bore without any objection. She didn't want to malign husband publicly. She thought of Ranbir only and lost love for elder son who became a rogue and was famed as prostitute lover. Wife of Sudhir shared grief with mother. Unfortunately she didn't bear a child till date and started having deep hatred for husband. She feared child born would have criminal mind. Her spiritual teachings revealed which was told in religious congregations attended by her regularly with mother-in-law. Two ladies started attending religious congregation frequently which was soothing and they became disciple of a renowned saint and made him Guru. They started going to ashram located in Hardwar and took advantage of long stay and bathing regularly in Ganges for solace and relief. They felt better and gradually gave up all luxury and adopted plain and simple life at home. They were addressed as Sanyasins. Life took a peculiar turn.

Ranbir followed Communist Philosophy for quite some time and one day he came in contact with Mina and proposed to marry her. The caste concept was not recognized by communists and Ranbir didn't care about this. They were serious workers and became full timers after completing their college education. Ranbir also completed his law degree and started practicing in town bar firstly to fight cases for cadre persons and peasants and additionally other cases. He started earning money and had comfortable life while wife worked in party office getting monthly allowance. Now they were not dependent on father. Their life was smooth and happy but never bothered to have a child.

2

Mother came to Ranbir after knowing his success as advocate and was welcomed. He firstly was shocked to see dress of mother and later understood when explained. His mother also came to plead for defending case of father, which he flatly refused. He didn't defend social offenders and wanted them to get punished. He was sorry to learn about his brother's issueless wife but kept silent after knowing her sufferings. She returned back to village sad but satisfied. One son was doing good work as educated advocate. One day again his mother came to see him when she was totally raked up and crying. "Your father has been issued a warrant of arrest for murder of a worker who was working in our land for last thirty years. He is innocent and murder was committed in dead of night when he was sleeping in house. I am definite, he didn't leave house and nobody saw him going to field. Now you must save him from going to jail by all means to protect our prestige."

"Why father himself has not come so that I could talk to him and find out details? Please ask him to come," son replied.

"What type of son you are that you don't want to stand by his side even in such distress? This won't be appreciated by anyone in society," said mother.

"I have not gone home for last so many years and he didn't care to know my whereabouts. Now you want me to see him. I have information both my father and elder brother hate me. I can't go and take any chance of getting assaulted by goons that he is keeping for doing all illegal acts," replied Ranbir bluntly.

Mina came back from her party office and saw mother-in-law crying on door. She asked her to sit. She didn't approve this type of behavior of husband who was rude to parents as if he was an orphan. She tried to understand situation and finally sought permission from husband to visit village.

She was having memory of her parents at age of five years when she lost them in a riot and got shelter in an orphanage. Ranbir gave a stern look and finally nodded. His mother came back with daughter-in-law home for first time. She met father-in-law sitting in verandah in front of house and gossiping to his hunch men and didn't bother about warrant issued for arrest. He looked at wife. "Who is this lady and what for she is here? Is she new helping hand to you in mismanagement of house? Where have you been last many days? She must be in Bhajan Group in congregation. I understand she must be singing well and pulling large crowd."

"She is Mina wife of Ranbir and your daughter-in-law. You never cared to see her but she has come to help us. Shortly police will come with warrant to arrest you for murder of Gopal which happened two days back. You're sitting and enjoying gossip as usual," replied wife being critical.

Sanad was perturbed for some time and cooled down while hunch men walked away. He was looking curiously at Mina and got impressed by her simplicity and beauty who looked so dignified. Mother asked her to go inside house. Father didn't know that Mina worked in office of Communist Party. He saw a group of labors coming to his house who enquired.

"Mina Behan has come to our village as some of us saw. Please call and we have to talk to her."

Ranbir's father was taken aback and wanted to drive them away when a commotion happened and Sudhir came out from inside and started pushing them away. They didn't move and he took out gun to threaten them. The crowd became angry and shouted slogans. They wanted to attack him. "Don't try to show gun. We know you have killed Gopal in field when he stopped you from assaulting his wife in field at mid night. Gopal wanted to rescue wife and you used gun and killed him. This was a big shock for father now who never knew that son turned into such a rogue. He could understand that his living in village was going to be difficult.

Hearing noise Mina came out and stood in front of crowd. One person said, "Behanjee this fellow has killed Gopal. Your husband is an advocate and we want justice for the woman. This man should be hanged without any delay."

Mina heard and replied, "We will ascertain facts and ensure justice to the lady. I am a guest here and came with mother-in-law some time back. You go peacefully and we won't hesitate in taking action. My husband shall also do the same. After all we work for all peasants and labors."

The crowd dispersed without a word and father was surprised to see such happening which he never imagined. Time changed but he remained in past days. Immediately he was worried to protect son from getting arrested and going to jail. In a short while police came and arrested him who surrendered without resistance. Mina also left immediately as she could know facts to be intimated to husband.

3

Sudhir was elder brother of Ranbir. In fact he was born when his mother was only fifteen, which was a tradition prevailing in villages where girls were married at lower age after puberty to protect virginity before marriage. Initially Sudhir being son of a rich man was pampered and got totally spoiled. Parents didn't care to check his habits and bad acts which gradually became more anti social. He developed into a man with loose character and started indulging in sex with young girls resulting in serious medical problems. His father suppressed these with money and got victims treated on his expenses. Poor villagers took it as right of landlords to exploit women at their free will any time at hour of day.

He was married early after he indulged frequently in scandals and confine to wife at home. His father couldn't be effective as he also indulged in wrong activities from time to time and family became den of scoundrels. Ranbir was born later after eight years and his mother took care not to allow him to mix with his elder brother or play. Sudhir could study up to high school but never passed examination and started working in fields with father and later handled all problems independently. He enjoyed this. He felt empowered when his father was confined to home and could do whatever pleased him. Ranbir was sent to school and after his matriculation he went to town to study in college. Sudhir with all his bad habits lost faith of wife and she also evaded physical contact and didn't have issue, which was a worry for father. They were planning to get him second wife declaring first wife as Sanyasin when Gopal incident came to light and father was arrested. He was very angry with mother and younger brother who took no interest in getting father released from jail. He realized the importance of father when workers in fields started revolting and refused to give crops putting family in trouble. He hired some muscle men and started punishing workers and engaging others for survival of family. He was aging fast and even at forty looked sixty and became a piece of hatred in society. His old friends left him and he was just a wrack not cared by mother and wife. He started drinking a lot and kept one widow in his house making her pregnant. He was forced to marry her by villagers. His first child was born from this widow and he felt relief and spent time with this child. Father was happy in jail on getting news of birth of grandson and celebrated in jail with inmates. Sudhir's first wife finally went away to stay in Ashram of her Guru and gradually became famous for religious preaching and developed own following despite limited education. She started earning money and built ashram for devotees separately. She acquired knowledge with help of guru and devotion to people in rendering social services which lifted her mental level.   Sudhir came to know about this but never thought to come in contact with her. His new wife of course once attended her congregation in town. She also visited Mina on her way back as she wanted to be in contact with family. In heart within, she felt someday she would need their help.

Ranbir's mother came to stay with him so that she could meet husband in jail from time to time and express regrets for all that happened. His father didn't want to defend himself to protect Sudhir even after hushing up Gopal's case with money. Sudha, mother of Ranbir was keeping all time unhappy and many times she stopped taking food which made her very weak and fragile. Mina got anxious and sought help of husband to convince mother to keep good health as father could get released any day from jail while case would continue.

One day Sudha got information about the mismanagement of property by Sudhir and also he was trying to sell land for more money. She rushed to village and tried to control. Initially Sudhir didn't object but after a short discussion lost temper and hit mother with a steel rod. Fragile and weak lady died on spot. He ran away from house without telling anyone in dead of night. Matterwas reported to police by neighbor. His wife Laxmi with her five year old son Romi went to Mina after police enquiry was over. But she was sent back by Ranbir to take care of property while son Romi was detained in town for study. It was for safety of boy that Laxmi parted with son and believed Mina and God to show the way. She was from a poor family and had little knowledge about property matters.

Ranbir's father came to know about killing of wife by son and regretted why he protected him despite knowing his guilt. Now he paid for mistake in such a harsh manner. He called his son and told him all facts about Sudhir killing Gopal who informed police to hold further enquiry. In no time fact was ascertained from same witnesses who spoke against Ranbir's father and bail was granted. This was better as old man took charge of properties along with Laxmi and started passing days. Now Sudhir was to be punished for two crimes and was absconding.

4

Sudhir after leaving home took a train and as beggar travelled to South and landed in a small locality. He found a motel and started working as waiter with full devotion to duty and impressed owner. He had realized mistakes and now wanted to be a good person. He grew beard as was common in new locality and identity for low grade workers. It made him hide face and he also picked up local dialect to mingle with people. His education helped him to become manager of motel after a few years. Later he became owner of the place as before death owner willed the business in his name in absence of any relation to be claimant. He refrained totally from drinking and womanizing and never uttered a word in mother tongue. He was already old and never thought of taking another wife and remembered son often. His fate took turn which was good for him. He was very lonely man crying many days in loneliness of night and sought pardon from family members.

He also remembered his first wife who left him and became Sadhavi. He remembered Laxmi more who tried to settle him in life even after knowing all criminal background and who gave him a son. Desire to see them again was full of perils when he could be caught by police. The local police was lethargic to act and there was none to press the case. Ranbir also ignored him having no personal interest. He was full of hatred for father and brother for all their deeds. He regretted and felt sorry for mother who was no more. He tried not to remember past and getting depressed. Ageing overpowered him gradually, but he remained active and alert to keep motel running. Many criminals visited his place for food and drink which he never refused for own safety.

Ranbir's father was equally disinterested and was counting his days to end life. He made Laxmi understand all matters related to property making her to own everything. One day he called advocate and prepared will where he gave all properties to Romi so that Ranbir may not be able to claim anything. This was a punishment he gave his younger son who neglected him and showed disrespect. But he missed Sudhir and sometimes worried about his being alive. He always thought him to be in difficulties and passing days. In dead of night he cried and reviewed own life thinking where he faulted and about punishment of loneliness he was undergoing. His life became burdensome.

In youthful days he didn't care for anyone even wife who also got killed under rage of spoiled son for which he was responsible. In fact he never tried to control his activities and spent time showing off his status and power to near and dear ones who exploited his wealth. He got filled up with bitterness for son and cursed, "Where ever you be, God must punish you". He also got remorseful for wife whom he neglected under vanity and high ego. Life for him became dreadful and full of pains. He became very sick and doctors could hardly diagnose his sickness and one day died in sleep which was found out by Laxmi in morning. She started crying and servants rushed to see. Immediately Ranbir was informed who finally came down to village after many years to perform last rites of father. He was sad but didn't shed any tears showing his anguish for the guilty man.

5

Ashu and Nina were not permitted to marry by Nine's father and were given shelter by family of Ashu, particularly mother and took great care of daughter-in-law. She felt comfortable and protected in house and forgot her parents quickly. Both continued education and became graduates with average results which could have employed them as clerks only. Ashu's mother didn't want Nina to work. The couple was also aggrieved and both decided to compete in administrative services examination. They vowed to show capabilities and worked hard. Nina also did household work and assisted mother-in-law to give relief which satisfied father. He also cared for her and brought article to run home smoothly at times when mother was away.

"Nina, are you happy with us? You shouldn't hesitate to ask anything required and I shall give you," said Ashu's father.

"Papa I am very happy. Kindly bless us so that we may be successful in examination and make you proud," replied Nina.

"You will definitely succeed and this is my conviction. Your Mother is not for this but she will also accept your success," assured father.

They appeared in examination and were declared successful in six month's time when results were declared. Nina was at higher rank in merit list of successful candidates and selected for administrative services. Ashu was selected for police service. Now Ashu's mother relented as daughter-in-law was going to superior class of service and she agreed to her working. The day two left home to go for training was very painful for both elders. Ashu's mother wept for long as she was to be alone again in house with husband. The couple drew satisfaction themselves that it was for a brief period after which they would be together.

They were sent to different places for training and separated forcefully. Both concentrated in training and ranked higher in respective services. Nina was placed in Delhi while Ashu was posted to Madhya Pradesh. They started working and mostly Ashu came to capital for official work and stayed with Nina and Ashu's parents stayed with her due to convenience of travelling to Meerut to look after their properties at intervals or whenever required.

"You know what attracts me most is your thick lips," and Ashu started seducing wife. They had a pleasant experience. They initially decided about no child before getting independent and keeping parents free from additional load of child care. Ashu's mother wanted child early and insisted regularly. Nina ignored smilingly without revealing her mind.

Ashu went back to place of posting happy and satisfied. It was Nina who earlier allowed all plays in bed but no sex in past days. She was equally happy and gave a very warm sendoff. Ashu's mother was having different brightness on face and she started praying God for good news at an early date. The news came just after a month when Nina confirmed pregnancy to them and extra care was in vogue. Ashu was scolded by wife for this outcome but internally she also was happy to become a mother. She was quite matured to bear child and perhaps it was most appropriate time. Ashu came to Delhi within a week to thank wife for news she conveyed over phone. Two were more concerned about new comer and spent time planning for child birth and care. They went to market and purchased toys etc for baby making mother overwhelmed and she also added few things to their list.

It was not very long when Nina gave birth to a girl child and their home was filled with happiness and celebration. Although Nina was new in service in the place where she lived, she was very popular among residents for her good behavior. They named child Swati who was accepted by all. The Child grew and borrowed features of grandmother but beauty of mother. She stayed with grandmother when Nina went to office and got promotions twice in last few years showing her efficiency and good working. In between she moved to some new places for working and got qualified for District Collector. She was also deputed to Bhopal, capital of Madhya Pradesh. Nina was having a great judicial sense in all cases and ensured none was given undue punishment. Also she didn't spare wrong doers and never paid attention to recommendations from politicians or others and earned some displeasure. All criminals in area of control were afraid of her toughness and which also became heart burning among them. They wanted her transferred back to capital in office from field. This didn't happen and she continued. Ashu was also efficient and developed special skill to handle ultras in state. He was made in charge of forces specially trained for the job. He was having a reputation of tough handling and relentless working round the clock. He now didn't get time to see family frequently. He went to see his daughter at long intervals who was now in a nursery school. He believed in care of wife and was least worried. His father expired in between and mother permanently stayed with

Nina and tendering granddaughter. Two were a pleasant combination who played and fought simultaneously and forced Nina to pass rulings. Swati was generally loser and thereafter they stopped referring any differences to mother. Ashu camped in forest and engaged in combing operations to control activities of Naxalite in area. He was all alone and felt about wrong selection of job. He was a soft person and emotional and would have been better in university teaching and doing research on these people. He wanted to quit and expressed desire to wife.

"I have started disliking job which is full of risks and extremely strenuous. Politicians are interfering in working and leaders of ultras are patronized by them," said Ashu to wife over phone.

"I understand your desire to be closer to women teaching in colleges and flirt freely. If all think like you who will administer state. These are very common obstacles and we have to find ways out. You shouldn't feel weak now. You are lucky that I take care of family without bothering you in any manner. You must prove capabilities as good commander of force and encourage them," replied Nina. Ashu was not happy with reply and grudged.

6

It was a bad day for Nina when she was informed by school authorities about missing Swati from school after lunch in midday. She was playing in school ground and someone allured her to take away to meet grandmother who was taken ill. This was told by children playing in group. Nina couldn't think that her reputation of a fair and just person should result in such happening. She talked to mother who reported absence of child at home. Mother started crying and asked her to find child immediately somehow after listening to news. Nina could also not inform Ashu whom she lectured recently on duty and couldn't contact easily. She had to face situation alone and silently. She didn't lose head and set in search of child silently after informing police for action. She wept silently in nights without letting anyone know. All her staff and subordinate were astonished on this extraordinary courage and she was dependent only on god.

Nina avoided publicity about disappearance of daughter and kept away from media. She thought publicity in media could endanger life of daughter more as they habitually made stories to attract audiences in larger numbers. Despite prevailing rules and restrictions they indulged in this and many times it became obvious that media misused freedom to make life of general public torturous and difficult. They in fact followed no ethics in working. Young reporters dealt many subjects and issues without acquiring valid information and tried to copy other competing media persons for scoring high. They changed details which threatened to fragment society. There was a free play and they also involved viewers from street who gave totally careless and personalized opinion. Ashu came to know about this and proposed use of force but was prevented by Nina. "See any use of force may precipitate issue seriously and life of child will be in danger. Persons who have done it want to take revenge from us. They might be facing difficulties due to our strictness. This is a negative part of our job and there are many others who are enjoying this painful situation. Even those who express their sympathies in long sentences and shedding crocodile tears can't be trusted. Our social norms have got distorted. All get entertained by scandalous stories and false brave actions of screen heroes. They may not stand even smaller blows in real life but come rushing to blame administration for all problems being faced," Nina tried to convince.

Ashu heard silently and restrained self from moving ahead. He thought "How my wife is more matured than me? In fact as woman she should have been more perturbed and disturbed. Is it due to different type of services we are in and trainings have been different? We have always been told to fight and face antisocial in society and that is basis of our total reasoning. He couldn't decide conclusively and was highly upset on fate of their child."

The two remained in poor state of mind and paid special attention not to speak anything in public despite provocations. They expected demand for ransom which never came and days passed by. Mother and Nina got more disturbed with every passing day. Mother fell sick and was admitted in hospital and Nina visited her regularly. This became additional burden on her.

7

The group which was involved in this was new outfit. They went to loot bank for getting money to pay for arms supplied from neighboring area. This was not in knowledge of Ranbir. These persons were commanded by a person who was veteran extremist and organized subversive activity many times without telling Ranbir. It was responsibility of leading man to recruit persons, train them and force to kill persons randomly to build criminal background. The objective was firstly to demoralize new recruit and secondly to spread fear in society. He had many informers from villages who were on role and paid them well. Same informers helped them to acquire latest arms and ammunitions even superior to defending government forces. They didn't succeed in looting bank as security forces got alerted by informer who was watching their movement. In frustration they picked up daughter of Commander of security forces pointed out by their man in public who was cadre member and local politician who failed to get elected in last election. Swati didn't cry on way and went silently obeying whatever was told to her. She always addressed them uncle and smiled fearlessly. It was surprising for group and they directly took her to Ranbir after returning to camp in jungle. Swati behaved as if she was visiting close relation and came on a picnic. Ranbir was astonished to see child and felt a different type of attraction and affection.

"What is your name baby? Ranbir asked.

"I am Swati. My father is Ashutosh and my mother Nivedita called Nina. My father is a police officer and mother is Commissioner. I was in school and playing during lunch time when one uncle came on plea of taking me to grandmother in hospital. But in place of hospital they brought me here. Please tell me where my grandmother is," she replied fearlessly.

Ranbir understood problem and called his personal lady attendant to feed child and get her new dress. He decided to take child himself to her parents but preferred to drop her in mother's place. He made a disguise to hide himself and travelled by a public bus. On the way the bus was intercepted by other armed forces. One of them identified Ranbir and shot him dead. Swati was left alone and taken by security personnel to Commissioner's home. None was there and finally they took her to hospital to grandmother. Old lady was very happy and took hold of Swati and asked hospital authorities to inform Nina. There was jubilation in family. This was a rare incident in realm of ultras activities. Nina didn't ask any detail and gathered them in normal talk from Swati. She informed Ashu about return of their daughter and simultaneously thanked God.

"The man who was bringing back child was none other than your father who was identified by security personnel and killed. He was in fact living with ultras in jungle after he separated from mother who finally died lonely after serious ailment. His group was eliminated but commander managed to escape as he got information about our action. You will be surprised that the group is patronized by leader of opposition in assembly who failed to win elections and failed to form government," informed Ashu.

"We know but we can't do anything if public keep electing these leaders and continue to suffer in return. These terrorists work for these leaders during election creating fear in minds of half educated people who are praised by same leaders for their political consciousness in many words. They also give money for future support. That is why I avoided publicity of incident and took risk of losing our child. I only believed on God to help," replied Nina.

Ashu once again felt outwitted by wife. He said, "I know you don't have faith in police force like many others who avoid involvement of force for peace of mind. Let me congratulate you as your faith has been winner this time too."

8

In days to come, Swati grew to be a very clever woman and preferred to be Professor in a college. Ashu supported her readily and Nina walked with decision happily. She was unhappy with life of parents who had taken premature retirement to run NGO for deprived children. They were running school for talented students orienting them to social development after completion of education. They sent persons to villages for educating in civil rights and duties. They desired to improve society and larger population with a view that someday greater awareness will spread to make our country worth living. Even now it is better than others in many ways. Awareness in green revolution, preservation of environment, conservation of water resources etc were included. Aim was to act for inclusive growth involving large industries and big business houses which now understood subject of social responsibility broadly and not merely funding school education, water supply, road repairs as part of this. Swati studied Sociology for Master's Degree in college and stood first. She also decided to do Ph D in this subject and covered area of Tribal's life and found out many details. She deliberated on reasons for increasing Ultra activities and failures of government which allowed its growth. The movement was being supported by neighboring countries indicating failures in international relation. It slowed down development of economy and country. Resources were diverted and many infrastructure projects were left incomplete and loss of manpower and construction equipment was on increase. The government couldn't control this effectively as federal structure of country was not responding favorably. State governments were looking in different direction than Central government mainly for confused working of political parties. Most of these parties were infiltrated with criminal elements who won elections on strength of money and gun. Under-privileged villagers succumbed to goons in order to save their lives. But they were highly exploited lot as all resources were plundered by them in various ways. Findings of Swati were critical and she faced difficulty in getting her Ph D completed showing that educational system was influenced severely by politics. Finally she got thesis published in foreign university which was highly appreciated. She was invited to work in university outside country. Swati refused as her parents left their jobs to work in NGO and she decided to participate directly.

Swati became close to Jitu in the university. In one seminar Jitu's oration impressed her greatly and they started dating regularly. One day she took Jitu home and introduced him to parents. He was a boy from an ashram for homeless and poor boys and brought there when his parents were killed in a major train accident. He couldn't see their bodies and cremation was done by government agency. Someone from government agency handed him over to ashram when he was only seven years old. He was good in studies and received scholarship in all years. He managed himself with money available and looked always presentable. None could tell that he came from such background. Swati was mainly attracted by his talent which parents appreciated after talking for few hours. After some days she expressed desire to marry Jitu which was agreed by parents. Jitu started living with them and became a strong support to family.

During Kumbha they together planned a trip to Hardwar when Jitu also went and as per religious practices offered Puja to departed parents and felt relieved remembering them on such pious place. In Hardwar one fine morning when Swati and Jitu got up in hotel, they found Ashu and Nina missing. They searched a lot and someone told they might have gone to other religious places of Badrinath and Kedarnath in hills. Swati was not aware of this plan and finally came back home and waited for their return from pilgrimage. But this never happened. Jitu and Swati returned alone to engage further life in activities of own. They handed over NGO to one reliable agency. They never looked back and after a few years went abroad to work in university together. The bitterness of life in India became a sore in their life. Now both partners were without parents and also homeless. They never thought of returning back due mainly to frustrating environment and utter self serving social setups. Their son Rohan, who was with them, became citizen of the country. Research and education was ignored in mother land and even if new ideas were given, it lost in bureaucratic system of numerous departments in government. They gave up hope of coming back and passed quality time with total professional satisfaction to earn many laurels in their field of work. Rohan later had own family and lived independently working as solicitor in nearby state.

Love is Forever

1

Raja got up early morning next day and felt highly confused. He was extremely tired from all happenings in last fifteen days and felt as if one life passed. He prepared tea to soothe tension of wife who kept sleeping late. He was back from his morning walk and didn't meet Sunni as usual. He thought man might be out of station and couldn't share latest local news and rumors of place particularly his case. He was preparing self to face situation directly in court. He felt low with happenings in family. He decided to give final push to pending case. Seena got up and took tea and kissed him, after a long time. He felt renewed love after long time and felt very close to wife. She smiled and started seeping tea from his cup. Later both shared tea for long time sitting close, while Seena slept in his lap feeling his excitement in cheeks. Maid disturbed them and both separated. She ordered maid to prepare breakfast after long time. Maid looked at madam and became serious and thoughtful. This was not liked by two. He was worried about suicidal tendency of wife and wanted to keep her happy not to face grave situation in conjugal life. He suddenly realized that absence of wife would make life very lonely and miserable. He would be forced to remain confined to avoid social embarrassment. He couldn't tell this incident even to closest friend or confidants who might propagate to make life difficult in society. What a constraint?

Seena got up and lazily walked as if fully under intoxication to bathroom and took long bath. Raja was alarmed and knocked on door to drag her out. She came out and tried to show anger but didn't see his long face particularly sad eyes full of tears. She wiped tears and assured him to be confident.

'Don't worry, I won't leave you alone but give company for long. I am already free from worries and know that you are my sole company in this world.'

'I am worried for your poor health and often falling sick. I think to withdraw case today itself and spend time peacefully with you. We may also go out from this place which is now biting me.'

'Why are you sounding so weak? You trust me. Everything will settle down fast. Try one or two more dates and then decide finally. I have no more attachment for final result in case. Even if you lose this property, we can buy another one.'

Raja felt comfortable and confident. He got ready and went to court. He sat in tea shop under big tree and watched movement of people around. He came early and later went to see head clerk who didn't pay attention for long time. He was getting irritated and felt like shouting on him for not giving attention. Suddenly he became status conscious and entered into realm of office power.

Then he changed stance and said, 'Sir I am back. Has any date been fixed?'

'You don't know that judge is in serious trouble. He has been trapped in murder case by police of Chennai where he took wife for treatment. Right now he is on anticipatory bail and in ICU. He is serious and may take long to come to court,' he replied in sad voice as if judge was no more alive.'I don't know what will happen to all pending cases. We are also dying hungry since last two months there is no earning. Mu family members don't believe us and charge that I have been wasting money. None appreciates our plight. Other colleagues are doing roaring business. Can you give money on loan for few days which I will return later,' head clerk requested. Raj was shocked to hear these words. He questioned, 'What about your salary? You must be getting this.'

'This is another problem. We are never sure when it will be paid. Treasury is not having money and government delays in giving fund. If one depends on salary, shortly he would be extinct. Also we are low paid and can't meet both ends. We live in same society and families and children demand all facilities they see around. If we question, family will drive us out from home.' Head clerk lectured.

'We understand that this has been our creation only. We didn't control in beginning and now it can't be changed,' the man was just at point of breaking in tears. Raj took out one five hundred note and gave him who pocketed it happily and thanked. He again said, 'I will try to give you back money as early as possible.'Raj walked away without hearing those words as he never thought to get it back and took it as donation. He was surprised on self for showing such benevolent gesture never done in past. He believed in "Karma" and advocated that all should get as per deeds and not as dole. He felt insulted after acting against his principles of living.

He reached tea shop and met boys working there. Owner was not visible and boys enquired together about his well being. They explained how they missed him every day for some unknown reasons. They also asked him not to absent for long in future. He was again confused what type of relationship developed among them. He sat down on chair and started waiting for owner. One boy brought a cup of tea which he sipped slowly and was thinking what turn case will take. In mean time the broker advocate came around and saw him. He spoke today in low voice and said, 'Professor sir, your case is going to be delayed for long as judge has fallen sick and is not coming in near future. The man is charged with murder of wife. Can you believe this? He is admitted in ICU in hospital and has suffered heart attack and blood pressure is fluctuating. He has eaten lot of money from public. He has been punished by God. I was told that you also had setback in your family. God should help you in getting favorable order from new judge being appointed shortly.'

'What was good behavior? He has been punished for serious guilt. Last time he wanted money from me to pass order. His clerk hinted but I didn't agree. I have been advised to move to higher court to get early verdict.' Raja was excited.

2

He kept seeping tea silently and didn't like to respond further. He felt a hand on his shoulder. This was tea shop owner and he turned head to look into his tearful eyes. He said, 'It was very sad to know what all happened with you and family. May God give you strength to carry on?'

Raja looked at him with wide opened eyes and could hardly speak. He was thinking how he knew all this and asked, "who told you?'

'Manish was here other day. He came to tea shop and enquired about judge who is involved in murder of his father. He found this out through own connections. He mentioned your name and said about your wife being related to him.' Old man said. He thought, 'Nothing can remain secret in life and nature has its own way of making it open. Many times we may not know but others know all about us particularly what we try to hide.' He kept looking at old man who perhaps knew many other things. Owner took him near desk and said, 'Now you may request for transfer of case to other court and early judgment.'

Raja never expected that Manish would act so trying to fix responsibility for death of father on judge. Second version was that his father was killed by an assailant by hitting on head with a rod while on way to hotel after seeing wife of judge. It was a dark place in street. The killer was intelligent to select place and mode of killing and also hiding his face not to get identified. His father was lying in pool of blood for hours on road. Someone walking on pavement saw body. He immediately informed police and also gave own name and address. Police asked him to stay on spot and not to touch body. They also brought forensic expert. The person standing there gave statement and expert took photographs and foot prints which were later found to be mixed up with that of man who reported matter to police. Otherwise they couldn't find anything which could reveal identity of killer. These all detail was told by Manish when he was back to home in Lakhnow while incident happened in Chennai. Manish knew that his father travelled by air only and disliked road journey. The purpose must have been urgent and someone informed about last wish of dying lady. This was informed by maid in ward, who sympathized with woman. She said, "The man told he was a judge and was worried losing daily income with absence. All men are same when his woman falls sick. He loves and cares when she keeps healthy and serves all needs. This world is highly selfish.'She asked Manish whether he was having wife. Manish informed that his wife was also seriously sick and he cared round the clock. Maid commented, 'You are gem of husband. God will save your wife.'Jaya recovered thereafter very fast and he could discuss with her about this incident.

Raja thought how Seena would react when she knows all details. He was still serious when broker advocate reappeared and informed, "Professor Sir, you know, Munna is roaming here. You may meet him if you want" He thought for a minute and gave consent. Munna was in his usual dress and came to tea shop for tea. Rohan was angry and caught hold of him. He started dragging him to court room. Munna couldn't get free from clutch of this elderly man who suddenly appeared to be a man of steel. He started shouting. Another fellow appeared from crowd and shot many rounds at him. He fell down on ground and all rushed to pick him up. They took him to hospital and Munna with his associate vanished. Police kept watching silently from distance and didn't move.

Raja was declared brought dead in hospital and his body was sent to morgue and police was informed. Court also got disturbed and people in premise were walking around. Tea shop owner was very much upset while his boys started crying loudly. Nobody tried to console them. Within hours tea shop started working in low key, which astonished many.'Professor has been shot dead. How this happened?' Head clerk and Peon asked old man.

'It was mistake of Professor who didn't remember that criminals move in gang and protect each other. He got excited and acted to lose life.' he replied in flat tone.

Old man informed Manish whose telephone number was with him and gave detail of incident. It was unbelievable and he rushed to this place. Jaya remained at home when told by Manish. He reached by evening and went to hospital next day and took care of body. Seena was informed by Manish who became silent for long time and was in shock. But she didn't cry. Doctor forced her to cry and gave pills to sleep and absorb shock. She was shown body of husband before cremation. Last rite was done in shortest possible time and it was over in one week. Jaya joined in this function and tried to console Seena.

Manish and Jaya asked her to come to their place which she refused. She decided to stay in her flat and spend time alone. But she was behaving normal and gradually mixed with old friends and made life easy within weeks. This was not appreciated by society around, which she didn't care. She constantly bothered about self and her future.

3

Seena one day went to meet ailing judge in ICU. He was looking fine and getting special care. Security was relaxed after killing of Raj.

'Papa why are you in hospital now? You should go home and rest.' Seena told him.

'Who are you? Why are you calling me father? I don't know you,' he asked.'I am daughter of that unfortunate woman who was killed in hospital in Chennai. I am her daughter and half sister of Manish. Now at least you may allow me to call you Papa. I have no other person in this world.' She was in tears.

Judge got up from bed and hugged showing normal condition. 'Don't worry; I will take care of you. Where is your husband?'

'He has been killed by a goon and associate of Munna.' She replied normal.

'It's sad but nothing could be done now. However, you come and stay with me if you want. I am alone now and often cry for my wife.' Judge replied.

An attendant of hospital came in room. Judge got upset on seeing him. He ordered him to go out. But he took out gun fitted with silencer and shot him several times till he fell down on floor and died. None heard bullet sound and no hustle were created. Seena ran out of room after seeing gunman and was hiding in nearby washroom for ladies. She was shaking for long and came out after police crowded the place. She silently slipped away and took an auto to reach home. She looked normal while getting down from and driver didn't accept money for journey.

'Didi I have done my job. I will be going out for a few months till case subsided and meet you thereafter. I have to tell you so many other things.' Auto driver drove away fast.

Killing of Judge in hospital became a headline next day in newspaper. Different people made different stories. One friend of Seena asked if she knew anything about the incident which she negated strongly. Her going and returning from hospital remained unnoticed. She never took any permission and went to room of judge casually when staffs were relaxing, primarily after death of Raja in court and was being discussed more.

Formalities were completed and it became news of past. Manish came to know all this and once again came to see her with Jaya. She posed normal and spent happy time with them. Once again Jaya requested her to come to their home.

'Jaya I am passing time remembering Raja. I didn't respect him when he was alive. I fought with him on every issue and disobeyed. He was a large hearted man who took my care and tried to satisfy all needs.' Seena revealed.

'I also hold him in great esteem. He was so kind to me when I was sick. But you are sister of Manish as both are having one father. You have right to take shelter in his home.'

'Raja has left this flat for me and also enough money in bank account. I am comfortable. I will come to you whenever such need is felt. I want you to take care of husband more and have happy time. "Loss of husband is a big loss" always remember this. I have decided to work in a voluntary organization for orphans remembering my childhood. This will satisfy me.' Seena became emotional.

Manish and Jaya left after spending day with her and she was again alone. She recovered by next morning and behaved normal.

She got up after a long bell by maid who came in time. One man was standing behind and she didn't recognize him.

'I am Joginder and friend of Munna. He asked me to meet you and enquire to know your welfare. He also said that you were looking for a driver for your car.'

'Yes but when you met him.' Seena asked.

'Two weeks back in Jalandhar this is his home town. I also stay there and operate a taxi company. I can find a local driver for your car.' Jaggi said.'I want a man who will take my car on monthly rental. He will operate and maintain this car and pay me fifteen thousand rupees per month.' Seena told.

'It looks to be higher. How old is this car?'

'This is hardly two years old and has run only two thousand kilometers. It won't need any major maintenance for another two years or so.' She clarified.

'What else?'

'It's in name of my late husband. Ownership can't be changed and it has to be run as private car. Driver will submit copy of his driving license and proof of home address as ID. This will make easy for me to contact him.' She told further.

'Anything else despite you made it all clear.'

'A car needs ownership change after death of Raja. You may get it done and engage any advocate.' She made it clear.

'I will get NOC from court in one month time through a known advocate who is very influential.'

'In such case you can find a buyer who can pay reasonably well.' She proposed.

'First let NOC come then you may sell car. In mean time I will find a driver who will be running the car as you want. This earning will help you to meet your expenses. I think you don't work.'

'You are right brother.' Seena said.

'You have called me brother and I will take care of you sister. I am impressed by your straight forward talk and simplicity. Note down my phone number and may call anytime in need.' Jaggi bent down to touch her feet and walked away.

Seena was surprised and asked maid her impression, who was standing all time while she talked.

'Madam you must try this man once or twice by giving some work. You shouldn't believe him straight way otherwise he may deceive. Such people are many in this city that is actually criminal.' Deepa said.

4

Seena told Deepa to cook breakfast and give tea. She kept pondering and walking in room from one place to other. Her inner sense said to decide in favor of Joginder keeping words of maid in mind. Two-in-one radio was very dear to Raja which became now her support. She played it all time while in house. TV viewing now scared her. 'Madam your breakfast is ready along with tea.'

'You are quick and also witty. You keep me advising now in absence of husband. I trust you and hope you won't misguide me.'

'You are joking. You are educated and experienced person. I am from village and can hardly sign documents.'

'But you have learnt more practical tips. I have lived as dependent all these days and enjoying earning of husband. I was never serious in money matters and wasted a lot. Raja warned me to be more conscious about spending money and advised to save in pennies also. I didn't like but now can understand wisdom in his words when he has left enough for me.'

'You will learn other things also very fast. I noticed the way you talked to Joginder clearly and keeping your interests intact.' Deepa said.

'He has called you sister. My experience says he will keep his words and commitment.'

Deepa went after doing morning work and returned again to cook lunch.

'Madam, watch TV which is showing the shooting of sir in court area. The man who shot looks like Joginder having beard and head gear.'

Seena tried to adjust TV but news footing was over. Now she had to wait for another time. Deepa next day changed and contradicted own observation. This change shook faith in maid and she was forced to think independently. Early next morning Seena opened TV and there was breaking news about death of judge who jumped out from third floor window in back side of hospital full of junk and refuses. The dead body was first seen by a cleaning man who had gone to collect his implements. He made a noise and immediately security persons rushed to spot and police was informed by hospital. It was sensational news and all channels were blurring stories with different theories and explanations. Hospital management was under severe criticism. Seena watched news with terror in eyes. She knew that shooting of judge was not being shown knowingly to hide ineffectiveness of policing. But she could do nothing to avoid own involvement and for long time trouble. There was knocking on door. Joginder was standing on door. She allowed him to come inside and closed door.

'Who are you? Are you the man who shot judge in hospital? Who gave you instruction?'

'Your husband told us to shoot judge who made his life miserable. He said judge had no right to live anymore.'

'You are lying. My husband was never such type of man. He was peace loving and couldn't think of such action. He suffered long for this reason only.' Seena said firmly.

'Why you shot my husband?' She asked further.

'This was our decision after killing judge. We knew he was a soft and simple man. We were afraid he could reveal our identity. He tried to take Munna to court. I couldn't wait long and shot him dead.'

'How TV is telling different story about death of judge?'

'It's Munna who planted story on TV channel and police wanted it to be done. Police would have earned bad name for lax security.' Joginder clarified.

'How you dared to come to my place and offer your services?'

'We were feeling bad about killing of Professor and decided to help you out of difficulties.'

'Now if I change my decision, what you would do?'

'Nothing as police wants case to continue forever. Judge is going to change and he won't take any interest. They are one in all such cases.'

Seena thought and said, 'You get NOC and buy this car which is not lucky for me. You may pay market price after getting car registered in buyer's name. I would suggest not to take it in own name which may go against you. You will also first get car transferred in my name after death of husband.' She dismissed Joginder finally.

She was extremely disturbed and decided to sleep. In mean time maid came and took order for cooking lunch.

'I saw Joginder. Did he come to see you?'

'Yes. He came to tell me to fight case with help of advocate and get NOC. He will come back after it's done to take car and pay price.'

'It's good for you.' maid said and went to cook lunch. Seena slept for long and woke up to take food. Maid went and she slept again. She felt comfortable after deciding about car.

5

Seena was feeling sad and finally decided to join NGO for orphans. She felt paying tribute to husband whom she couldn't understand till he lived. Now he looked a hero, who revenged death of mother in similar way. She was calm and rested long for day and night.   Deepa felt that she was going to lose her mistress shortly who looked withdrawn from life. Now she felt soft for her and considered well before talking to her. Earlier she was very tough and arrogant and always pricking on smaller issues and often using foul language. Deepa had sympathy for Raja who looked to her a perfect teacher keeping mostly busy in reading and typing on laptop. Madam often fought with him for keeping busy on laptop and didn't take interest in her. She wanted to be playful and naughty like younger woman. She often used abusive and vulgar words declaring him to be an impotent man not able to sleep with woman. She also charged him with affair with maid in her absence from house. He in turn hit her and punished for such behavior and later wept for long alone.

Deepa was from village and heard use of such dirty slangs by elderly women there. They fought and she kept away from house whenever it happened.

Joginder returned within few weeks and gave money for car. Seena took money and within a week went to same hill station after marriage for honeymoon. She easily located the lodge and stayed in one room to relive past memories. Room was by side of the one where she stayed with husband after marriage.

Her stay was pleasant and she often peeped into side room just to feel presence of dead husband. She felt like being invited. One day she went and slept on bed when it was open. She found it soothing and got into deep sleep. It was evening when the occupant of room came back. He was alone and came with gifts. He was taken aback to find a woman sleeping on bed. He doubted some ploy and called attendant to ask about woman.'

'She is occupant of next room. By mistake she came inside your room and was resting. We thought her to be your friend as many come with girl friends to have greater enjoyment. We didn't disturb her. Now I can wake her to go out.' Attendant said.

'No let her sleep. I shall go to dining room to eat and come back. By that time she must be awake.' Ritesh told attendant.

Ritesh returned in one hour after enjoying songs of a popular singer in dining room and was highly impressed. He sang romantic songs liked by him and remembered wife who sang them. His wife died a few months back living him alone without any child. Back in room he found Seena sitting on bed. She recognized Ritesh who met during honeymoon days and spent intimate time with her while husband was lost in reading books. Now once again they met and old attractions suddenly revived. It was unusual for newly married couple but happened. Wife of Ritesh was very lazy and mostly rested in room. Later days two couples spent time together and made joint programs. It was interesting that Seena and Ritesh stayed together while Raja entertained wife of Ritesh. They separated after holidays and promised to meet again. This happened now after two became singles again.

'How are you? We are meeting after many years.' Seena asked Ritesh.

'I couldn't recognize you while sleeping. It's very surprising.' Ritesh replied.

'Where is your wife?' She asked.

'She is no more and expired few months back after long sickness. I am alone now.' He replied and in turn questioned, 'Where is Raja who was very pleasant and sporting person?'

'He was killed by a killer when he went to peruse a case in court despite my serious objection. Of late he turned arrogant and never listened to my words. He started disliking me. I am now alone.' She narrated in brief.

'You know you were sleeping in my room and not yours.' Ritesh told.

'Yes because this was my room when I came with Raja for honeymoon. I was finding this very comfortable and slept well after long time. I felt presence of husband.' Seena said and expressed regret for inconvenience caused to Ritesh.

'Let us make this stay like honeymoon this time also. You move to this room and vacate yours if you don't mind.' Ritesh proposed instantly.

'I will be happy to do so. I love your company and care. We can relieve our love of those days when we came with our partners. I am very lonely and feel unsafe. I am afraid I may also get killed by goons who killed my father and husband.' Seena told and ran into arms of Ritesh. They held each other long.

The attendant wanted Seena to go to her room as she came into wrong one.

'Let her be here and she will stay with me. She is my old friend and now would be wife. We have decided to get married in court.' Ritesh pronounced looking at Seena. 'You shift her belongings here while we go for a long walk on lonely roads like other newly married couples.'

Seena informed Manish and Jaya about her decision to marry Ritesh. They asked her to wait for one day and travelled to hill station. They witnessed marriage of two and organized a dinner for all inmates in lodge. There was dance and drink and publicly Ritesh kissed Seena for long as requested by guests. Jaya and Manish couldn't believe their eyes about Seena getting into fast life. Now they knew why she was not happy with Raja, who was a simple man with old manners.

'Congratulations Seena for picking up a man of your choice and have a very pleasant time.' Jaya told but Manish kept aloof and felt sorry on turn of events suddenly. Jaya consoled him.

'Thank you Ritesh for sheltering my half sister who met incidentally after long time after killing of my father. Please take care of her and in case of any need you may call me.'

Old couple with new tie up stayed for three months. Seena sold flat and went to big house of husband, who was a businessman. He owned wealth and took her around world on business trips. She learnt business and became a good advisor to husband. After long time she became pregnant and proud mother. This was a medical exception. They lived together to care for child and have a pleasant time. She finally got engaged in rearing child and grew her family.

'Is it possible to have a child so late?'

'Exceptions are part of nature and it happened for happiness of this couple.' Doctor replied without giving detail.

Rehabilitated

1

Life of Vidhu became abnormal after death of wife. He worked under severe mental trauma not knowing why he couldn't save his wife. He kept office timing but often missed breakfast. He locked room of deceased wife Mona where she committed suicide with overdose of sleeping pills. He cursed why he was careless not to check her habits being sensitive police officer. Why he couldn't see serious incoming damage to family peace? After all Mona was wife whose behavior changed due to neglect she suffered, he felt. She came often late in night and absented many nights and returned drunk in morning. She became addicted from a teetotaler and lost all charms. Why he allowed drifting by not satisfying her normal physical needs? Did he become cold and started hating her silently?More he analyzed, it blocked his reasoning and senses. Many times he broke down and sobbed in dead of night after servant Ramdin left to rest in backside room where he lived with wife and came only in morning to serve tea after walk. His morning walk was regular when he thought without interruption and got clarity in thinking for working in office. But by evening he was again engulfed in darkness not to emerge till morning. It was a surprise how he was not losing health generally seen in such cases. "Vidhu, I find you unhappy at home. I can understand reason. You have to bear with this loss. Don't forget that Vibha is dependent on you and if you keep detached, it won't be good for young girl. Please pull yourself up and start living normal. Your wife has been punished for wrong she did and you needn't worry," spoke Ramdin who addressed him by first name and felt close. He was serving him since childhood.

"Ramdin Kaka, I don't find mistake done by her. I took all care to provide everything that Mona wanted. I never came in way and always thought her to be happy. What went wrong that she had to end life? I find myself guilty for what has happened. Vibha won't pardon me for loss of mother."

"Yes you were at fault. You didn't understand that woman is like fire. She was full of limitless lust and greed. She lacked common sense and couldn't understand worldly happenings. Her interactions were limited due to low education. A few close friends easily influenced her with bad habits. With limited interactions she thought self quite wise and became overconfident to face cruelty of society and was misled." "It is job of husband to keep a watch and control wife from time to time. This may look stupid but remember if fire is not controlled it spreads fast and damages all. Some clash of interest and views are bound to happen and create ugly scenes. This needs to be adopted as woman gets out of sense fast and can create ugly scenes making life unhappy. This unhappiness is also at times necessary for healthy and happy days and children grow in balanced ways," Ramdin lectured.

"But nothing of this type happened forcing me to be harsh or unpleasant," said Vidhu.

Ramdin smiled and said, "You forget that you never questioned her for absence from house and also how she spent nights. Why she stayed out for whole night? One morning I went to give tea, I saw Mona half dressed and drowsy and inviting me to bed. Thereafter, I never went into bedroom in morning and always considered Mona Bahu. You never checked dresses she used and increase in alcohol consumption. You also didn't question her absence from house all night and that she was involved in adultery. What a poor husband you have been?""You never in fact took interest in her and allowed her to pick up friends freely. You pardoned after knowing about costly necklace she got as gift. What were the occasion and why anyone should give but for some favor or pleasure? Nothing comes free in this world and one has to pay for everything," Ramdin was excited.

Vidhu couldn't say anything and moved to bedroom to absorb what he heard. He sobbed for long to get relief till Ramdin knocked door and came with water and tea.

"I am sorry Vidhu for all harsh words I told. But this should take away burden from your heart and mind. Remember life has to go on for fulfilling future responsibilities. In your case it is Vibha which should bother you now. Mona has gone, take it as a bad dream," told Ramdin and walked out.

Vidhu took some time to come out of room. He bathed and dressed for evening walk and informed Ramdin. It looked he overcame agony and was prepared to go ahead. He only thought about Ramdin who knew all happenings

in family which he never bothered to know. He also knew
about all bad habits of Mona. He probably knew about
advances made by servant which Mona confessed a few days
before ending life. Mona was really trapped and was a timid
person. Any other bold woman would have fought and dealt
strongly. Perhaps she was not confident of support from him
as he kept silent even after her confession which was sign
of a courageous person despite all wrong deeds. He didn't
find courage to console and render support in getting her on
right path. She must be frustrated from activities of bating,
adultery and money making and desired support of husband
to come up. Vidhu once again started blaming self as timid
person and couldn't overcome his background from which
he came up. He took a longer walk that day and found
Ramdin pacing and looked worried. He became normal
after seeing him. He was anxious that long unpleasant talk
might put troubled man in further difficulties. He applied
method like a surgeon to take out bad blood from wound
to help in healing.

Vidhu took dinner silently and went to bed with a book
to read before sleep as a habit. This was normal and Ramdin
felt satisfied. He knew his responsibility to tender this new
patient and his increased moral responsibilities. He became
a true guardian for him who lost parents long back and was
having no brother or sister to support in difficult times.
Ramdin went to his room and prayed before God for some
time seeking strength to carry burden which he picked up
on his own. He also shed tears for sad and troubled man as
if he was his own son in trouble.

He recalled days when he used to roam in household of
Vidhu's moving behind father and asking many questions on

subjects of interest. His father was a patient man who never lost temper even if he committed mistakes and his master also supported. He said, "Never try to kill initiative in a child who learns better by committing mistakes. Teach him to be attentive and careful in working on anything. Always give responsibility and allow freely working keeping an eye on safety and damages likely to happen. Child becomes responsible fast and he turns independent in working at very young age."

2

Ramdin became dependable at the age of six years when he started rendering personal service to Vidhu's father such as arranging things for bath including few buckets of water, placing his sleepers and washed clothes at assigned places, filling tobacco in the smoking pot after meals in daytime and also in evening. He also took care of guests serving them with water and snacks from inside house and never left any place shabby or dirty. Ramdin's father was very proud of son. He also sent him to village school to study where he performed well showing extraordinary intelligence and always scored high marks and top rank. But he never forgot to serve Vidhu's father after coming back from school till he retired in bed and Ramdin went to sleep with father on verandah. The session for wise words started while in bed when Ramdin's father taught good manners, stories of brave people etc. Also at times experiences on conjugal life and problems between wife and husband were described by father mostly in gossip session with mother. This was a typical learning and many times his mother stopped father when he became too elaborate keeping in mind tender age of son lying by side. She dragged her husband inside the room for completing the gossip but generally for physical relation. Ramdin slept in between before his father returned to bed by side of son. Later when Ramdin grew further he could interpret actions and felt shy. But this was also learning for him. He practiced this when he was married and lived in room given by Vidhu. Ramdin remained without any child making wife unhappy. He underwent medical tests and found that his wife couldn't bear child. Finally they devoted their life to Vidhu and Mona. It was only Ramdin's wife who told him all that was happening inside house and she was critical of Mona who was ditching her man. Ramdin was reminded by wife all time to take care of Vidhu particularly after death of Mona. The relationship grew closer. Ramdin's wife never talked to Vidhu directly and moved away from his way if sometimes facing him directly.

One day Vidhu spoke to Ramdin's wife when he was very sad after death of his wife, "Kaki why you don't talk to me? I am very lonely and feel like crying all time. I want you to be close like mother who has already left me. Ramdin Kaka is like father and he loves me. You also behave like him in present situation. You will have to take care of Vibha now whose mother is no more and left us alone. I want you two to stay inside house like parents and guide us to live now." He was prepared to be guided by an uneducated woman for being happy.

This request didn't go unheard and one day Ramdin and wife moved inside house to take care of troubled man who was constantly cursing self for the mishap. Life went on slightly in changed way when all time vigilant eyes of old couple took good care.

3

Ramdin's father was a leader of poor agriculture labors working in fields and tried to defend them in case of any injustice and got their problems sorted out. Vidhu's father was not bothered as reasonable person and took good care of people working in his land. His activity in labor welfare increased when Ramdin started caring for his master. Many times he accompanied his father to these meetings where he heard silently to discussions and appreciated father's active role for which he earned respect in working class. He also went to discuss matters with authorities and got their appreciation. He also attended court cases and slowly got recognized as leader of working class. He became the District level Secretary of the organization and later member of the main body of labor union. All these days Vidhu was studying in town and finally competed in civil services examination to get selected in police cadre. It was recognition for family. In village one by one his parents expired after sudden sickness when he couldn't be present. He blamed himself for neglecting parents and got totally absorbed in his career building and family. Later he sold all lands in village and asked Ramdin and his wife to stay in town and places of his postings. Some land was given to his father for his working and livelihood.

Life in Vidhu's household became drab and monotonous and everyone talked less. Ramdin and his wife gossiped long about him and his sad life after death of Mona. Vidhu was not able to rid himself of blame for suicide by her. His belief in self diminished each day and he felt that sleeping of servant in bed while drunk was not a serious guilt to end life after getting flirt. He would have punished servant in different way. It came down to him only negligence of wife for career. His office work also slowed down and many times boss and colleagues pointed out failures in office. One close friend in office told, "Vidhu I can see that you are very sad after demise of wife. You are still very young and it will be difficult for you to pass whole life like this. Now a few months have passed and I will suggest you to get married again. Your daughter has also grown up and after some time she will settle down and get married. After that you will be lonelier. You must think about this to have a normal life and it's not difficult. There are grown up girls getting married late or you may also find a suitable widow with minimum liabilities."

Vidhu looked at him with no reaction and went home for lunch. This idea stuck in his mind and gradually he was out of deep grief caused by death of wife.

Vibha was coming in holidays starting shortly and he decided to first talk to her who was matured for and could decide. Even otherwise also she gave many ideas in family life and professional work including office work whenever asked. He found those ideas very practical and workable. She demonstrated high maturity when she came after getting news of death of mother a few months back. She cried for some time but controlled after seeing pains of father. She wiped her tears fast and took role like mother guiding in daily routine and cared to remove sadness quite often. Vidhu thought his dead mother reappeared in family to support and console in this moment. Ramdin and his wife were also surprised and appreciated young girl for many actions at time of agony. She could stay for a short period as classes were already going on and she couldn't miss them when examination was not far off. She now felt doing well in study and settle down fast to keep father free of worries about her future. Vidhu felt sad to think about her going but couldn't stop and was lost in self. New idea of getting married again was proving to be lofty and pleasant and his dreams started hovering in mind and life. He suddenly started planning for honeymoon after marriage and resolved to take more care of new wife. He often got lost while sitting in living room or in garden in evenings.

This change was observed by Ramdin and once he said, "Babu I am really very happy to see your changed mood. May God always keep you so and tell me what I can do to keep it so." Vidhu could hold and replied, "Kaka one friend of mine in office suggested to get remarried. What do you think about this?"

"There is nothing wrong in this situation when wife died at an early age because of some reason. Your grandmother was second wife and mother of your father. First wife died during child birth as those days medical facilities were not good. After death of first wife your grandfather brought second wife in house who was a decent lady and took great care of Dadaji," replied Ramdin. Suddenly Vidhu felt relieved of all worries as he wouldn't be doing anything wrong and he could easily convince Vibha. Next moment he started thinking if new woman made his daughter's life difficult, as normally seen. Why man becomes more docile to second wife? Is it that her demand on person enhances in a big way or he feels highly obliged for agreeing to marry? This is universal and many families suffer in this way. But there has been exception when second wife has put family on path of progress and betterment with her skill and tact and made considered and experienced moves. May be it is individual what matters rather than general. In the mean time Ramdin came and Vidhu asked, "Kaka it is found generally that second wife makes family life difficult and problems increase. Is it true?"

"No it is not always true. I know many cases when second wife has done well to family and its members provided reasonability is not lost. New person can't solve all problems. Remember she would also be a human who is likely to fail in difficulties and must be accepted," was the reply.

Vidhu was satisfied and he went for evening stroll which he had started after getting enthusiastic about second marriage and its positive outcome. He didn't want to appear before new woman weak or in bad shape particularly with pot belly which had grown in previous months due to depressed mood. Perhaps he was eating too much to kill time and keep his mind engaged. He slept less and body gained weight. Medical science has done a lot of work on this and suggests healthy thinking and worry less life is important to keep body in good shape. Vidhu was now particular about two time walks and regular exercise while keeping watch on weight. He intended to impress his would be wife as if he was marrying for first time. He also resolved to take better care of new wife and not to neglect in any way which he did to Mona. He felt a twitching in heart for Mona and desired to cry for some time in one corner of room. This was not possible as Ramdin and his wife always shadowed him while in house. They were also happy by his changed mood. They were behaving like serious guardian him. In fact environment of house was filled with positive and pleasant thoughts which were missing for long.

One morning Vidhu got up early to get ready to go to the station. Vibha was coming after finishing examination. During this period she was not disturbed by any member of family and generally "everything is well" message was given hiding condition of Vidhu. Now it was better and they were confident that she won't be able to know bad patch already spent. Suddenly there was knock on main door while Vidhu was still in bathroom and Ramdin found Vibha standing. She signaled him to keep silent and sat on sofa. She picked up photograph of her mother kept on corner table and started crying silently. Tears were rolling down on her cheeks uncontrolled. Ramdin and his wife got bewildered and couldn't decide any move. They stood fixed in one corner and kept watching. Many minutes passed when Vidhu called from bed room to announce his going to station directly through the corridor. Getting no response he peeped into sitting room and was aghast to find Vibha sitting on sofa almost half fainted. He didn't know how to start his dialogue and his own eyes were in tears. Last time when two met they had no time to talk to each other and also he didn't like to show his weakness before daughter. Life becomes so difficult at times, felt Vidhu. It was only Vibha who got up and ran to grab father and started crying loudly filling room with grief and sorrow. He also kept shedding tears and finally sat down on a chair while his daughter sat on his feet keeping head in lap. He tried to console by caressing her bob cut hair, which she got trimmed to express loss of mother who always suggested keeping short hair and she never agreed. Again life forces many change and living styles get altered unwillingly with some incidents.

Ramdin came forward to pick up Vibha from floor and made her sit by side of father and spoke words of consolation sympathetically.

4

"Death is the only thing which is certain and bound to happen. When and how it comes is not known to anyone. We have only to try living in best possible way keeping check on habits and behavior. Our forefathers have been preaching and teaching ways to make life more relevant to living conditions and pass days in working and doing well to humanity. Then person passes away a satisfied soul and others revere his days." Ramdin told as senior to Vibha. "Your mother was a brave person and took all care of your father and family. She was full of love and compassion for family members and particularly she loved you so much. Her days were limited and she passed away in sleep as if her heart ceased to function. Doctors also didn't say anything and it was considered a natural death. Sometimes secret diseases also take away life." He said further. "Nature does its work while we freely enjoy life and ignore many symptoms in excitement. Calm down and settle for peace for your father who has been suffering alone all these days after demise of your mother. We didn't want to disturb you and hid many details. You may pardon us for this deliberate action," told Ramdin in continuation expressing long experience.

Father and Daughter looked to each other and finally got up to go in their rooms. Vibha occupied mother's room which was no more used by father and spared for wife to be alone when they entered into disharmony and life of differences. It was known to Vibha and she was not comfortable in bed of mother and couldn't sleep easily. She felt some unknown hands were extending and trying to touch her body while in sleep. She got up and started pacing room and avoided going out which could disturb father. Finally she went to take water from cooler installed in kitchen. While passing in front of father's door she heard him talking to someone and heard voice of Ramdin who was discussing in low voice.

"Vidhu today morning a lady telephoned to respond to advertisement posted in matrimony column few days back. She is interested to marry and wants to meet you in person to discuss detail," Ramdin informed. "How can I talk to her till Vibha agrees to this proposal and she must be taken into confidence? If she doesn't agree I can't take any chance to make daughter unhappy who later will hate me," said Vidhu.

"We must give visitor time may be after a few days later while we talk to Vibha. You will have miserable days alone particularly when she shall get married and go away with husband to raise her family," said Ramdin.

"I feel she should be informed about suicide by mother particularly after servant episode which forced her to end life. Her extra marital activities should also be known to her so that she can accept remarriage in right perspective and to avoid future hatred," told Vidhu.

"It will be too intense for young mind and I feel so sorry. But who can change destiny. I feel she is more matured and down to earth than we think and will adjust fast with new situation," said Ramdin.

Ramdin prepared to go out of room when he crossed by side of kitchen where Vibha stood shocked with a glass of water which she was holding in hand. He enquired, "What happened?""Nothing I was thirsty and came to drink water in kitchen," replied Vibha."I was also too tired and now I would go to sleep," Vibha further said and went inside room and fell on bed. She sobbed for long not knowing when she slept and got up late. Father had gone for morning walk. She got ready quickly and took bath not to show her real mental condition to him and take tea with him when he was back. She prepared special breakfast of father's choice and served him. She also took glass of juice and two slices of bread.

"Papa I think you remarry now to get settled in new way and quickly. I can see that you have become very sad and lost all charms in life. You can't spend time like this which will be bad for me also," said Vibha.

Vidhu was taken aback and immediately remembered words of Ramdin yesterday night. He silently finished breakfast and quickly left for office without responding anything. Vibha went back to room and once again wept and slept long. Ramdin heard girl and also saw her crying through opening in door and felt very sad for poor girl. He thought about bad luck that forced her to bear all these unpleasant situations at young age.

She kept sleeping till Vidhu came back for lunch with her, which generally he took in office sent from home. He went to room after a long time and felt remorseful when many pictures passed through mind and being prominent that of servant sleeping in bed with his dead wife. He closed eyes and walked back. By this time Vibha came up to hold him affectionately and glanced lovingly. This made father happy momentarily. She said "Papa why you are looking so sad. Forget all past happenings and live in present. I knew all about mother and her affairs told by her. One night she narrated to me as friend firstly in excitement and subsequently broke down later narrating all her immoral acts. She went into depression and couldn't sleep for long. She got up and took many pills to get sleep and got up late in morning when you were gone."

"You knew all this so long and still behaved normal," Vidhu looked shocked.

"Not only that, once she was out for whole night when I was at home during vacation for few days and she returned home totally robbed. She was smelling alcohol and disoriented. She had taken drug in party. Her purse was full of currencies of high denominations. I didn't dare to ask and understood she was beyond mending. In fact I went back to college that very day telling Ramdin and making excuses for an urgent work. Back in hostel first time I got drunk alone. I was restless for many days and controlled by my friend with difficulty and roamed around with close friends and visited religious places and prayed only for your peace. I cursed you for high tolerance and restrain you showed and never opened up," Vibha became emotional.

"Why you have returned to this wretched place? Why are you talking to me? I don't deserve any sympathy as couldn't keep check on wife who drifted before my eyes. This is no love but blind faith in partner to get in serious problems. What is the use of success in career when family goes disarray and finally permits suicide?" Vidhu started crying like a baby.

"I heard you and Ramdin talking last night and in morning suggested remarriage. I can't see you in agony and pain which is not your creation only. Mother got wrong genes and she easily drifted to wrong acts not accepted in civil society of ours. I again request you to normalize as matured man, understand such happenings being done under greed," she tried to conclude.

Vidhu was practically dragged by his daughter to dining table to take food with her and asked to take rest before living for office. She engaged herself in afternoon to reset bedroom of mother removing all articles and photographs. She destroyed many gifts by mother and gave away to other families working in house. She gave all clothes to maids and their family members which were costly. He was thinking that girl must feel married new and not second wife to father. This could make life comfortable and easy.

5

A new advertisement was inserted by Vibha in matrimony column giving truthfully all details about father. It was so convincing that within a week two three proposals came. She sat down and responded in order of preference. Vidhu was now not keen to get involved particularly in view of facts revealed by daughter. He was not able to face daughter boldly and thought about likely ruined future for her. He showed nervousness but obeyed daughter without questioning He went through the detail and consented decision of Vibha.

The first lady came and couldn't impress Vibha as she was very fashionable and her showing off attitude. She appeared dominating which could put father in trouble. The second lady came with her father who talked less but interfered and didn't allow lady to speak anything. Third lady named Ruma came who was decently dressed and looked from rich background. Her dress looked modest but elegant. She was soft spoken and talked in selected words and controlled tone and with self respect and decency. She divorced husband as man turned out to be a criminal and batter and forced her to free socialization with friends and their wives. He intended to grab wealth of her father. One day she filed a divorce petition alleging husband to be loose in character and a womanizer. She fought case and won. Now she was free and intended to settle in a respectable family not of businessman but bureaucrat to have peaceful life. Vibha truthfully explained how her mother lost life in depression and sickness but didn't mention about suicide. Vidhu also talked to this woman but couldn't make up mind and burden came on Vibha to decide in consultation with Ramdin. Everything happened fast and court marriage took place in presence of small group of family members and friends. A reception was done in hotel to give social stamp to marriage when no old friend of previous wife was invited. Both father and daughter were satisfied at end of it.

Vibha was impressed by new mother and she became close friend quickly. She spent few days and went back to college to peruse study. She promised mother to be back early in next holiday. Household was well set and it didn't take time for Ruma to adjust with all in house. Vidhu became sad after departure of daughter and Ruma took his care. He was indebted to his daughter for settling his life fast. The setting of room was changed and Vidhu was back in same bedroom which was big in size and located better. The life moved on as usual.

Vibha returned happy but she became sad when memory of mother haunted frequently when alone. Her mother lost character and got into a bad company to lose track, but she couldn't get detached absolutely, who spent nine months in her womb and lived on blood in her veins. She was having some haunting dreams never seen earlier when mother advanced towards her in sleep and took to lonely place never seen earlier. This terrified her too much and she got up from sleep after listening to complain, "Your father neglected me and he didn't understand my needs. I was all time lonely and went to friends for passing time. They misled and I indulged in immoral acts. All teachings of my mother vanished and I cursed myself constantly and consumed more and more drinks. Some males exploited me in that state. You never get into this my dear. This makes life terrible and you fall from your own eyes to suffer all time." She frequently cried in nights and got up in between getting disturbed sleep. She also couldn't pardon father from whatever happened because he became selfish and neglected wife. Her emotional needs pushed her to friends who in turn got her involved in easy ways of enjoyment. They also gave money and arranged rich customers. In fact she was very attractive which her father could never know. She started hating men in general particularly husband who tortured wives and made them unhappy for progressing in career. Vibha kept disturbed and life got totally upset. One day her friend Atul came after holidays. Vibha ran away early from home not finding it comfortable despite vouching for change in family.

"I came to check whether you returned from home. Is everything alright in your place? Are your parents doing well?" asked Atul.

This was sufficient to break her hold and she started crying and Atul consoled and calmed her down. There after she narrated happening at home but didn't utter anything about mother.

"I feel sad about loss of your mother who is always dear to child, whatever she may do. She also misses child and suffers internally without expressing openly which gives pain. After all bondage of nine months nurturing through blood can't get washed by external happenings in life," said Atul.

"But remaining in closed door may not give relief. You come out to see around happenings in city and society and many activities may attract attention. You start thinking and pondering painting pictures for life and decide ways to go. You are having many classmates who are here only and didn't go out from town." Atul informed. "One day I saw Lina and Sina in market enjoying ice-cream and then went to a thriller movie recently released. It's good entertaining movie if you enjoy actions and loud sound of guns," Atul tried to push her to normalcy.6

There after he said good bye and promised to visit some other day. He also asked her to keep talking to ease mind and move away from painful absence of mother forever. He thought about complexities of world and particularly society. People gather to rejoice and get close and associate to enjoy more. Then also they come together to mourn death and separation. Isn't this our own creation to draw pleasure and sorrow in sequence? Vibha got up and took bath and dressed to go out. She checked up with Lina who was in market along with Sina and invited her for pizza lunch. This was after long time to eat pizza she liked. In fact she had a weakness for this junk food. She hurriedly went to place told by Lina and met them outside Pizza Hut. They went inside and took a table. The bearer came and took order without any delay. They did this to entertain more customers. Lina was looking at Vibha intently and getting anxious.

"What has gone wrong with you? You look being sick for long. You had been home to see parents. Is everything alright there?" Lina asked without pause.

Vibha's eyes were filled with tears but she controlled not to create scene. She had been weeping constantly since last two days after returning from home. In reality she missed all meals and survived on some cookies and biscuits and stored in room and ate noodles in between. She didn't wash herself properly and took several quick showers without soap or shampoo to cool self. Now she narrated all that happened in last one month. She also told about remarriage of father on her initiative to remove his sufferings and sadness. In turn she suffered and detached from home. She was sure not go back home soon as new mother might dislike. Father will try total control on new wife. Humans are extremely selfish lot and some do social service projecting as reformers with intention to get into politics or making more money with collection of fund from public. They also squeeze government and bribe officials to make happy and going further in their plans.

"Where are you lost, come back to face reality. Life is bound to end for all who are born. Yes, but early death is shocking. Your mother must be sick for long which you never knew. Your father was extremely caring type and never refused money demanded by you. What suddenly went wrong," asked Sina.

"Is it that your mother committed suicide due to internal bickering with father which you may not know being away in hostel?" Lina thrust this question without caring."Yes" Vibha broke down "but none knows reason including father or old time servant."

"Vibha come on, pizza has come and eat it fast before it becomes cold," said both together.

Vibha was feeling light after talking to friends. She enjoyed pizza after many days. She looked calm after eating. Lina said "We will take you to a new place in evening which we visit frequently to relax. You will also be relaxed for night. We will come and pick you up."

Lina came around eight in evening and found Vibha pacing in room. She was ready and eager to go and morose feeling was gone. In fact she was looking charming and attractive. They took an auto and met Sina on way. They entered a house and were welcomed by a smiling young man as if he knew their arrival. Inside they sat in richly furnished drawing room of a wealthy man. Gradually around a dozen young men and women gathered and all were dressed in latest dresses revealing their body curves. Vibha was surprised and looked to Lina who signaled to be easy. Some drinks and food were served which Vibha found tasty but different. In very short time her head became heavy and she went to washroom and felt her legs shaking. Lina took hold and safely brought back to seat. Vibha wanted to leave but Sina asked to wait for some time. They all were led to an underground hall which was full of smoke of marijuana.

Vibha didn't like the place. Lina and Sina forced Vibha to smoke pipe. She tried and after one or two pull started enjoying. Vibha found a boy making advances to her. Sina pushed fellow back and took her out from there. She was still jittery when back at home. She slept with difficulty and got up quite late in morning. Atul came in morning when she was still under influence of drug. "Yesterday I went to a place with Lina and Sina and got very late. I slept for long and could get up when you rang bell," said Vibha.

"It's already noon and also lunch time. I came to take you for lunch as you will try to give it a miss," said Atul.

"Give me some time I will change," She requested. Atul was not happy with the incident. They selected a small place to have simple food which was not tasty to Vibha. Both kept silent and ate.

"Vibha don't go to any such party where people are unknown just on invitation of friends like Lina and Sina. These are not good girls. You may get into trouble and repent for whole life," advised Atul.

"What is left in life? Mother has gone and father has remarried. Where shall I go in case of any need?" She asked. "You can't spoil life and also some other life trying to be close. Imagine how your father will feel when he knows you took drug? Atul talked like mentor.

Atul said "You had gone to a Rave Party yesterday night. I never knew that Lina and Sina go to such parties otherwise I would have stopped." "We can stay together till hostel reopens," he said further.

Vibha got alerted by name of rave party as she knew it spoiled young people. These basically were places to pick up girls and pushing them into sex rackets. She slept again and got up late in evening awakened by Lina and Sina. Vibha refused to go with them. Sina tried to press her and she became angry and slapped both and drove them out. She was upset again. There was knock on door and she opened door to allow Atul in. He came in and saw condition of Vibha. He spoke, "Your two friends are standing on road with their boyfriends on turning. Are you ready to go and join them?"

"I have kicked them out few minutes back when they tried to misbehave." Vibha said in anger."I am having headache and slept for long. I am still not normal and would like to take more rest. Should I make tea for you?

"No. I was passing this way and thought to check you. You need more rest and better take some food and go to sleep which is necessary. Vibha closed door and fell again on bed. Her body pained by cruel act of two wild teasing by Lina and Sina. She was scared and locked door firmly and slept. She got up when felt hungry and ate all bread and jam and gulped lot of water. Next day Atul took Vibha for lunch in a different place and spent peaceful time while eating. Lastly she asked "Tell me if you can marry me. I can't live alone now.""Let us first complete our course and then we shall go together to seek permission from your father to marry and have happy life," replied Atul

Vibha further said, "I feel good about you. We will make a happy couple and live nicely. Failure of father will never recur." "Vibha I promise to marry you and go to your home to meet parents and seek their blessings and live together." Atul repeated his resolve."Fault doesn't lie both in wife or husband. It's a failure of two partners when one becomes more greedy or over enthusiastic in some areas forgetting pious duty of family person. Both are responsible for disturbed life." Two concluded. Atul held her and kissed and caressed. He dispelled fear from her mind and finally went to meet Vidhu who agreed to their marriage. All mental agonies vanished and two lived and worked to live well. Finally they had a lovely son born in due course making all happy. Ruma proved to be a very responsible grandmother to her child.

Turmoil

1

Swami Shradhanand was highly revered by devotees gathered in Hardwar for taking dip in Ganges from all parts of world. Foreign devotees spent months in his ashram where every evening there was song and dance. These included modern tunes popular with youngsters. Many young girls and women were lost and forgot themselves. It was said that drugs were also consumed by them in one corner of Ashram known to authorities and police never attempted to disturb. Plain clothed policemen enjoyed in gathering which became free for all late in night and was big attraction. It was distortion of religion but no civilians dared to speak against. Anyone talking against or bad were dealt severally and many time publically on some excuse. Still Swami was popular. He was known for his preaching full of practical tips for happy living while remaining spiritual and mostly talked about loyalty to nation and its pride. Today he sat calm and quiet for long since early morning which signaled deeply set remorse of high magnitude in personal life. He could hardly sense happenings around and suddenly he jumped into river to save a group of men and women who were taking bath in ice Cold River and lost hold on chain put for safety while taking dip. All bathing persons formed chain and entered water together holding each other's hand and decide to cross barrier normally not allowed by volunteers. It happened within minutes while Swami was just watching flow of water and lost in of own thoughts. He saw floating group and jumped to save particularly one woman whom he knew but not known to his devotees. He caught her hand also which Samanta saw but was of no use. They together were swept away by strong current of water. The bodies were recovered by rescue team seven kilometers downstream away from place of mishap which included body of Swami. His body was deformed and full of injuries which surprised on lookers. On his left arm name of Susmita was engraved and perhaps was woman whom he tried to save. He recalled the name that met in town ten years back and was a renowned artist and sang in very sweet voice in gatherings during festivals. He also performed last rites as known person of this woman along with all other and was joined by many youngsters. This was considered a pious deed when one acted to give respect to deceased persons. Pundits did rest and fed all poor beggars and destitute without any discrimination. Swami's body was taken by disciples to perform last rites in different way which also he saw and a pang of pain went through his nerves as if he was his close relation. He became very sad and started analyzing whole incident and was lost in thoughts for long time. He couldn't conclude anything in particular and thought about irrelevance of life which he lived proudly and struggled to earn wealth and gained in many ways even troubling others. He was remembering Kamta who didn't come and kept busy with her son and his wife.

He thought "Every life is a journey when he keeps moving from one place to other and meets different sets of people while visiting places including religious ones which motivated to do good to people. These places of religion are set with all basic facilities required for short period stay and one gets opportunity to learn new things about life and people. One many times gets inspiration to change habits for peace and also future prosperity.""These places surprisingly solve many riddles of past life and one may find long time missing dear ones unexpectedly. This is termed as special favor of GOD. Religious gurus exploit situation to build own empire. They adopt particular way of life and study books of religion and use writings to explain and elaborate them for masses intelligently showing their analytical power and also gather experiences from meeting disciples to frame stories to tell next group.""They promote Selected Followers who join disciples and provide shelter etc to keep them in fold. In return followers keep on giving donations in money and materials and they keep growing rich. There is no Dharma involved as generally understood; but none the less it can be seen as pilgrimage. Swami was somewhat different even allowing free love and free mixing in pleasant ways. He never prompted and all happened voluntarily." Samanta pondered and looked sober and finally tears rolled out from his eyes.

"All of us take journey everyday and next day is never same. New work is picked up for prosperity and better living. One may think too intelligently and also understand for long. But every person changes physically and mentally every next day and there is some internal renewal taking place. People are busy struggling to survive and small change goes unnoticed." He continued explaining self."For example own spouse changes every day to behave differently.

Some day she is very pleasant with good understanding and next time very selfish and conflicting. This happens because she changes by a bit everyday with experience both good and bad which gets stored in inner self and is difficult to wipe out. That's the reason every advancement is different journey." He tried to conclude.

He couldn't get rid of thoughts and continued, "Working life and places are also type of changing stations in journey when one gathers new thoughts and ideas to operate working conglomerate better and in efficient manners. We invite different experts who worked in many companies in past and listen him and implement ideas with confidence and accept visitor as superior entity with new knowledge and higher experience. In homes also we pay attention to elders and listen to their thoughts carefully to find if something useful is being said and use them for better future." His thoughts became clumsy and unclear."We respect our teachers as they give us knowledge and facilitate advancement from nursery to college and thereafter. We never hesitate in accepting short term engagement to gain something larger and positive." He delved into own past."Everyone tries to stick to chosen path but at some stage gets pushed to destination unexpected and steps into wandering and searching something exciting. It becomes different type of pilgrimage. Some of these may be disgusting and still is undertaken to quell stresses and control strains. Some others use religion as shelter for benefits and exploit pilgrimage as plank for building groups and organization. Many anti-socials and criminals gather. Corrections are desirable with determined and clear mind." Samanta was back to present. He didn't give up but tired mind wanted break. He looked to sky to get further energy as an old habit. He expected new ideas coming from serene surroundings where crowd was busy bathing in ice cold water.

2

Hardwar is place where people from far and distant places gather on selected dates and times in a religious ceremony with friends and family. The crowd is huge and administration prepares for this festival for long. This is occasion when unscrupulous elements also assemble to wash away their past deeds and purify themselves from all sins committed. This belief has been prevailing in society for ages and in generations and ritual continues. It must have been started for purpose of seeing country and get tagged with religious rituals. Many people came to pay homage to departed souls of family members and for salvation and securing place in so called heaven. This is when people silently realize that end of journey has begun and one must do good things in society and purify selves. This was worked out to keep elderly busy while doing no job for gains or earning. Exceptions could always happen. Ladies dropped all fashions and costly attires, giving these to younger ones coming after marriage. This again has changed now when elderly women became more fashionable and indulged in immoral acts to satisfy urges and needs. They wanted false appreciations on their look and wore costly ornaments to show wealth in public. These groups also came to this congregation in name of religious ritual where actually they preferred to show riches and fashions. Many sex workers came to entertain customers and earn fast bucks. The society changed faster than expected. This population was not so large earlier but activities easily drew attention for interested many to participate. River Ganges is worshipped for this also along with supporting social needs. Nature is great absorber of so many happenings in society.

3

Ankit and Nirmala came to take bath in Ganges on pious occasion of Full Moon day, supposedly very sacred for any couple who wanted child and also well being of living kids and their families. They stood for long in ice cold water and felt relieved from tiredness of journey. They travelled from Mumbai by road in hired private car. This was craziness of Ankit who often ventured into long journeys on roads to different parts of country. He was member of Adventurer Club of city which was having more than five hundred members. They worked in own companies and some were billionaires, who never took risk. It was only small group of people who were more active. Other rich persons supported their venture and financed trips. They set certain missions. This time it was, "Saving Leopards." None knew how this subject was picked up. One day in a monthly get together story was narrated about leopard entering in one residential area which forgot ways. It was confused to go out. All efforts were made to trace and drive it out. All failed including men from forest department. They were sitting in one place totally tired and lit fire to keep leopard away. Suddenly it jumped from tree just nearby but didn't come close. Bullets were fired and beast was being driven back to jungle nearby." But the path it chose to go crossed main road. Rows of speeding vehicles stopped it to cross road. While crossing road it got hit by a laden lorry and was injured. Wildlife people picked up this animal and took in a jeep to hospital. It injured some rescuers while being pushed into vehicle. They tied it with rope around so that it couldn't move head. ALL forgot to give water to injured animal. As a result it lost sense and kept lying in hospital premise. Doctor was supposed to come from outskirt of city and was caught in traffic jam. Doctor came and checked and declared it in serious condition. He tried his best to revive but couldn't save the animal.

Ankit was one person in crowd and passed on message to his group. Leopard finally died and dead body was handed over to forest department to complete formalities. A case was filed against persons who brought it for treatment.

It took five years before case was dropped when Justice took exception on working of administration. Ankit and friends took up project of "Save Leopard". Initially Nirmala was against this activity but finally Ankit won over and got her nod to be active. Government wanted to give a financial aid which was taken to strengthen movement. Public was involved and everywhere volunteers worked and coordinated and shared details. This time administration was alert particularly on this occasion as there was dense forest not far off. Millions of people were visiting this place in couple of days. Other arrangements were also made like parking of vehicles, stalls for food and also for puja items required to worship river. There were other deities mainly from family of Lord Shiva. It was nostalgic in many respects and one could enjoy when visiting and bathing in ice cold water not available anywhere else. One felt comfortable after taking first dip. Certain freshness in body and inner self started flowing. After bath one wanted some sumptuous dishes like hot Kichadi and sweet dish of fresh Jalebis, the taste of which stayed in pallet for long time forcing desire to stay longer on bank. Several rounds were eaten by Ankit and wife and all days were spent on riverside. Guest house was far and they came prepared for whole day and both travelled by rickshaw pulled by man. Nirmala hated this conveyance but accepted as this was source of livelihood of poor coming all the way from villages. She always paid without negotiating like others,

She said, "Why people pay gladly heavy bills while eating in restaurant and give tip as well? But they all find it as saving by reducing payment asked by such hard working men."

Aarti of Ganges for more than an hour and was special attraction, pleasing and soul filling. One got lost in beauty of river where lights reflected and scattered all around. Even ordinary looking females also looked beautiful divine. Inside feelings got evoked added by onlookers. Many youngsters picked up love partners to have good time for lifelong. It worked as solution to prevailing problems in marriage of girls. Chanting mantras and singing song with drum beats made moments soothing and added to emotional motives. Ankit met Nirmala remembered their first visit after their marriage and didn't find any change in intensity of pleasure. This time their son accompanied them. Surprisingly he kept aloof from them from day one and picked up own timing of coming and returning back to guest house. On that eventful day both came to take bath, which was annual ritual. It was not possible to say who attracted whom. This was debated by two even now who advanced to embrace in an isolated place in street under a dark lamp post. Their parents were left behind when two walked faster just to get some privacy. Nirmala was attracted and Ankit acted like grownup male holding her tight. This activity finally ended in guest house in night when all slept but they remained active.

Morning they sighed for some time looking at each other which evaporated with warming of day. Nirmala avoided privacy now and felt more guilt to surrender. They returned back home and hardly met. They never cared to collect address which became problem in days to come. Nirmala started observing changes in self and also became worried. She couldn't tell mother who not only reprimand but severally punish for the act.

"It's a pleasure to see you here in our house. Where had you been? We remembered you often for all help that you gave during our visit to Fair in Hardwar." Mother of Nirmala questioned.

"I was busy in study and examination which are over now. I thought to see you people during recess after examination." Ankit replied.

"What course you are studying?" Father asked.

"Now you must spend some days with us. Nirmala has completed her school final. She is getting bored. You may take her to Delhi for few days and show her city." Father suggested.

"Let me ask Nirmala. She should be ready to go." Ankit told.

"Yes why not? I will call her." Father said.

In few minutes Nirmala was before him. Both moved away to private and isolated place out of house. She told him about pregnancy and wanted to get rid immediately. Father's proposal of visiting Delhi came to their help and both travelled to city next day. They searched for a doctor for getting aborted. Doctor refused despite knowing them being unmarried as it was delayed. Finally they went to a private nursing home in remote place and got free.

This incident was noted by one staff who worked there and started threatening and demanding money to keep silent. His demand increased day by day and one day finally both vanished from city and reached home of Nirmala. She looked pale. Mother expressed concern when daughter made excuse of serious sickness putting Ankit in difficulties and made their trip boring. Mother's experienced eyes understood what happened. But she felt happy within for daughter.

4

Ankit came back home and went to college. He felt guilty for all that happened. He resolved to complete study and then marry Nirmala after getting some job to support her. This again didn't happen and she was married to other boy in neighboring village. Ankit received message and consoled self. He was extremely frustrated and unhappy. On completing degree he joined armed forces and went for training in Military College. He became Captain in Sikh regiment and was posted to northern border. His life changed but in nights he often remembered her.

He came back in holidays to village when he received news about Nirmala becoming widow. Her husband was killed in a road accident few months back. He went to see and console the family.

"It's good you have come. My daughter has suffered a blow at this young age. She has stopped eating and keeps crying. Only you can console her as old friend." Father spoke with tears in eyes.

"Don't worry I will try to do something to remove her grief." Ankit replied.

Two met again after many days in a room inside house. Mother gave him eatables inside. Time passed in silence. He was to start talking to her when mother came in and closed door.

"Son only you can save my daughter. She told all about what happened between you two. You should have told me earlier and I could have set everything right. Now she has become a widow and none will marry her. We are in real difficulty." Mother started crying.

"Please don't cry. Let me talk to Nirmala. She is Indian wife and may not like to remarry. We did mistake initially and to save her dignity we went to doctor. I had a mind to come to you after completing studies, but you got her married. I didn't disturb and joined army to keep away." Ankit got emotional.

"What do you want? Will you marry if he agrees?" Mother asked.

"How can I spoil his life? He is a respectable army officer and I can't malign his name." Nirmala spoke slowly.

"Don't worry about that? I will make parents to agree for marriage as they are now pressing for this. In army such marriages are given equal respect and none will talk about this." He tried to convince.

Mother looked into eyes of daughter when father also joined and intervened.

'This is a golden opportunity for you my baby. You will get back your love and spend time well." He said and broke down. Ankit felt highly embarrassed to witness such scene. He never imagined father crying before children and wanted to run away.

Ankit advanced and held her hand and vowed before parents, "I am ready to accept you as wife. I will come back with parents to marry in a simple function. You may make arrangements." He left half happy and half in pains.

He returned back after a week with his parents and two more relatives. Marriage was organized in nearby temple and priest issued Certificate of Marriage which was registered very next day in court. Nirmala was handed over and they went away. Parents of Nirmala felt some bad dream was over but cried for long to drain accumulated stresses carried for months. They became normal very quickly, a normal human way to 'live and let live'.

Ankit and Nirmala couldn't have any child. Doctor said this was due to damage caused to womb as result of forceful and wrongly done abortion. Two accepted responsibility and never blamed each other. Nirmala now became sporting type and fully involved in all activities of wives of Officer's Club in army camp. She became Secretary of club for many terms and became popular. Ladies passed gala time during her tenure.

One day news came that a newly born child was abandoned in back side of hospital in garbage bin. Nirmala decided with consent of Ankit to adopt this child. They named him Samanta. He proved to be bright child and later studied well. Ankit as senior officer now ensured all facilities to him and child progressed well.

5

Samanta started a durable products outlet in his home town where Ankit helped him to buy a property. He lived on first floor while his showroom was located in ground floor. It was running successfully but he was unable to appoint any person because of limited income. He met Kamya one evening in market place. She lived alone after separating from husband. Husband was working in a trading company and was ditched in business. He also used call girls to get orders and shared cut. This impressed him. He offered job of manager to her. She accepted and impressed him by her smart working. Nirmala came to know about this and rushed to check activities of son.

"Who are you? I am mother of Samanta and stay in army camp. Tell me about your background and family." Nirmala posed questions in absence of son.

Kamya paid her respect and said. "My mother is working as nurse in hospital. Father is a small farmer and works in village. They found a boy who was sales manager in a private company. I am MBA from institute in town and was married to that man. He was hard working but corrupt which I knew after some days. I asked him to stop and try to live within fare earnings."

"It was good but why you decided to walk out of marriage?" Mother asked further.

"I came to know that he also supplied call girls to client to earn business and higher commission. This I couldn't tolerate and without delay I left him." Kamya talked peacefully.

"How you met my son? Did you ask for job?" Mother quarried.

"I was also stunned when he offered me job after knowing my qualification and very next day started working." She replied.

'Where do you stay?" Mother enquired further.

"I have been given one room with attached bathroom on one side without disturbing privacy." She responded.

"How often you meet my son in a day?" This was next question.

"We meet only in show room Mom." Reply was given by Samanta who returned after visiting a client wanting to place big order."You are questioning like a police from this simple girl who is already a victim of duress given by husband."

"It's interesting son. You have started defending Kamya without knowing much about her. She may be wrong. If you plan to marry her, she has to divorce husband." Mother clarified.

'I know mom and know rules well. She has already applied for divorce on ground of 'Moral Blows' by husband." Son told.

"This is unheard term being made ground for divorce. We discuss these problems in ladies club where advocates are present. None mentioned this ground ever describing cases." Mother expressed strongly.

"Mom ours is a new world and we want different ways to deal with situations and problems. Your days have gone which may not work now. We wish laws to change for freedom of woman and man can't exploit her forever. She has left husband on ground of immoral practices and court has to take note of this." Mother realized strength in logic given by son.

"Alright when are you coming to meet Papa who is missing you for long. He couldn't come due to his engagements and sent me to check you up." Mother patted cheek of son and walked away without waiting. She wanted to do few more things in town before getting back home.

6

"Your son has become a reformist. He has engaged one woman fighting her divorce on moral grounds. Her husband indulged in immoral practices in business. He must get into trouble one day." Nirmala reported to husband without remorse in voice.

"After all he is my son. You recall how we met and finally got married when you were in serious trouble, although own creation." Ankit replied.

"Do you think he wants to marry this woman?" She questioned.

"My sweet and simple wife, it's obvious. He is not a fool to get into trouble of getting her free from previous marriage unnecessarily. Secondly he has put her into respectable position. This woman will grow his business fast and control better, I can bet with you." Ankit said smiling.

"This is your bad habit to bet on anything and everything. This you have learnt from army culture. One day you may also bet that you never slept with me and put me to medical examination. You are really a hardened mind man." Nirmala got annoyed.

Ankit took her in embrace for long to make happy. They stopped discussing matter when they didn't have much to say. New generation wants to do things in their ways and old generation must keep watching. Any interference may jeopardize normal relationship.

It was not long that Kamya got divorce on same ground. They came to Ankit and mother to seek permission for marrying. They agreed instantly. They got regular feedback from son on case which was made onetime almost impossible. The decision came after a woman judge came and heard matter seriously. Many criticized but Judge never took note. Kamya called her parents to request formally for marrying daughter to Samanta. This was celebrated in simplest possible manner and very few guests were entertained. Later the new couple threw a party to important clients and their families.

7

On that eventful day Samanta saw Swami who was trying to save woman from getting drowned and lost own life. He realized that it was same as he did with Kamya. She was with her mother expecting baby after many years. He came to accompany parents and ensure their safety on river bank.

He looked above into sky and tried to see if his real mother or father was visible who left him in garbage bin many years back in hospital. He looked at couple who saved his life and finally got him a respectable place to live and develop family. They also passed through troubled days as told by mother one day. He felt highly blessed today. These souls only keep world running despite many injustices faced and given by men in different ways. "Freedom comes after many tests in life" Samanta finally thought. He got up and walked to guest house to check if his parents were safely back.

Troubled

1

Early in the morning Ratan got ready to go to institute where he worked as professor of business management. He taught Ethics which was interesting for him. His wife Sita hated this subject from core of heart. She knew how her papa made a lot of fortune as a surgeon by operating patients on minimum pretext and charged heavily. This was mandatory for hospital where he worked to increase income of the place in which he was paid forty percent of hospitalization charges in addition to consultation fees. Money was no consideration for Sita in father's house and they normally went to shopping where they only signed the bill to be settled by a man from doctor's business who also generously made money. She only knew how to spend and never thought how difficult it was to earn. In late evening doctor's pet subject was to narrate, 'how he convinced a man to get his stomach operated without waiting for long medicinal treatment and enjoy life'. This he narrated for hours before contingent of five daughters and youngest son. His wife was fed up with these stories which accompanied at least four pegs of whisky of lower brand while superior brands were kept locked by his wife in steel chest with a fear that someday any child may get tempted to consume.

Doctor laughed and said, 'I never knew about drinks and now I drink like a fish, how? Have you ever thought about it?' Begam today I would be true in confession to you. "It's a story when I went England for higher studies in Surgery. I met one woman who became my close friend. She entertained me regularly and also brought housewives who were her neighbors. They all encouraged me to indulge in such activities. I was habituated and became a womanizer. My father got me married before I went for study. But new association was very pleasing and all were fantastic." "You are good for producing children but not good for enjoyment due to your restricted thoughts and lack of freedom. I asked you many times to try this liquor and then you know pleasure of living." Doctor was turning vulgar in talk when wife drove children away and walked inside bedroom. Doctor was served food by servant and slept in adjoining room attached to bedroom which invariably was locked from inside by wife. The life in doctor's household dragged this way and his wife accepted all and she was left to take care of half dozen kids, their education and most importantly marriages of all five sisters. Sita was the second child and good looking and matured to understand all that went on in parent's home. She carried memory when her maid brought neighbor to entertain and collect good amount of money. She confined into her room till man left. She picked up other bad habit of prolonged gossiping and always criticizing others for some reason or other. Her craving for money was insatiable and made life of husband tense. Once or twice he was pushed to verge of official enquiry when she directly ordered costly items and got included in official bills for payment and supplier also added items of own need to bill which was caught by audit.

In his previous working career in business he always stressed on ethics in business organization from personal to professional. His friends made fun of him and called him old timed man talking in line with village seniors and avoided discussion with him. He had weakness of becoming emotional on these issues.

"Look you will earn rich dividend in form of moral strength and face anyone doing wrong. This could be very strong personal strength to face all odds.""That's the reason you were left behind in getting promotions as your bosses avoided you and gave low ratings in confidential reports. I have heard your lecture in classes on new appraisal system you delivered well. I think you should leave this job to become a teacher which will suit you more. There you can teach all moral values to students." Sita taunted."We have studied for earning more money to serve family needs and our parents are always looking up to share more," said one of many friends sitting in canteen to take tea during recesses. He retorted friend by making face as if some bitter substance went into mouth. He was showing hatred to my adamancy and perhaps cursing "God will punish you in life all the time, you over smart guy. He will take you to hell."

"You are also right and my parents also want money. They want me to earn over and above my regular salary. I give them all savings many times making wife and children unhappy. I can't buy a costly gift and she looks with tempted eyes to shining ornaments of friends and expresses frustration at home. I am unable to convince that it would come in time," replied Ratan in sad tone.

"Friends, why do you cry and make yourself sad, when river of money is flowing by your side? Just gather at your convenience. Only you have to have courage to do so. But always remember to share this with bosses and close associates from time to time who can come to your rescue.""They all are experienced people and know how to manipulate or reply when questioned by investigating officers. Keep reserve to feed enquiring man also as all expect when questions are raised. Any numbers of logics don't work where money clears your path and it becomes free of obstacles for future. Have you heard that lubricants are applied to reduce friction between two bodies coming in close contact," suggested second friend without reservations. He also cited many names and examples which Ratan already knew.

This was not the first occasion when he received such preaching. He remembered once when he went for inspecting supply in outside city and supervisor came and gave a closed envelope and politely said, 'sir boss is not here and only this much money is with me. Please keep this.'

'Why are you giving this to me? I came to do the job and now like to move from this place. I have to catch evening train. You keep money as company pays me enough salary for my needs. Don't ever try to bribe without checking character of a person visiting your place with such business? There are a few like me who don't like to take money as gratification.' Ratan was highly annoyed.

"Sir this is customary in business and after all you travelled long distance leaving family at home who must be expecting some gift. This is normal and even we do so when on tour. There are persons visiting who don't take money and buy costumes and dresses for family and bills are paid by us. This I can't do as boss is absent and also we are given limited freedom," man talked shamelessly.

Then one more visitor came who was company representative located in city. He was received with great respect and given a seat. I moved and fellow showed courtesy to say bye outside office. He had no appreciation for whatever happened moments back. He finally said, "Don't mind sir. This officer of your company has come to collect share for this job as he spoke to me in morning before you came like other times. Yesterday he made us pay a heavy bill for another visiting officer of company and also collected his share. This is the business custom and we realize this expense from you only through short supply or defective supply." The man explained without fear. He walked away silently without looking at him and also not responding to his gesture. He was full of disgust and contempt of different type never experienced any time earlier. His thoughts ran, "Who is corrupt and who makes system corrupt?"

One day he received a call from user department officer raising alarm, "The box is carrying items inspected by you and some stone pieces and less number of items. Would you like to check yourself?"

"No. You please report short supply as packaging was done in my absence and the supplier be black listed immediately." He replied harshly. The officer telephoning closed line. Once again it was a very sad moment for him. He was happy not involved in bungling. Later he enquired from officer who complained and said. "Supplier was informed and he replaced those boulders to make up short fall and your suggestion to blacklist party was opposed by chief saying, "If we start punishing suppliers like this who is doing business with us, one day none would serve us. I don't agree to such madness.""This supplier has always been very reliable and may be some worker played this mischief. The person may be our own man opening package. He is very polite and treats supplier well visiting office. It seems he didn't serve this time well and got annoyed." Boss clarified.

This was another shocking experience for him. He was scared that insisting on action may result in getting framed in any case. Thereafter, he refused taking even tea with suppliers on some excuse not to reveal his internal fear. He felt, "In the corrupt system man playing fair is a highly perilous situation."

"What happened and where are you lost. Tea break is over and we should be back to work," suggested friend. Internally he decided never to practice anything to get immoral and his confidence returned and others looked low in his eyes.

2

Ratan's morality increased with passing days which reflected in all office dealings and bosses were scared with his straight and tough talking. They took revenge by commenting low performance in confidential reports and rating remained only good. His promotions were delayed and every time he was left. Sita mocked and later children joined chorus "Most upright man in family". He didn't surrender and uttered, "Promotion is not everything in life. Uprightness is more important and one will certainly be fully compensated if hard work is continued." His wife brushed aside his saying, "Those who fail to get promotion in time always talk so." Ratan kept cool and got busy in work which he liked. He preferred doing any work big or small with own hand. Many times he did simple plumbing and electrical fixing work in house and saved money. He also washed dishes and retained this principle of self dependence and respect for all work.

In morning he got ready quickly and prepared own breakfast of toast and one egg omelet to keep check on cholesterol as suggested by doctor and took a cup of milk avoiding tea or coffee. He restricted his tea and coffee intake as he sat for hours on chair preparing for lectures. Earlier practice of working at home was objected by wife, 'I am not a show piece in house. I am a living being with all senses and need attention and care now after serving you long years during service period. Also I have produced two kids for you which I never wanted. Always remember this house is mine and you have to now follow my orders and fulfill all my desires." Her pitch of tone changed to shrill. She coughed often and he rushed with glass of water to smoothen dryness in throat. She looked at him pathetically and later smiled.

Once or twice it was ignored with smiles but after repeated happening Ratan thought it prudent not to show laptop which one day she threw on floor. Thanks to robust design that it wasn't damaged and, thereafter, it was kept inside bag. He took permission for operating this when required and she slept after lunch. Also he worked late in night even after satisfying her which obviously made her happy for the day. Morning was a busy time and tea was made by him. Sita lied on bed till late hours and he completed his morning walk. He played sticky lover role in morning trying to push and at times lift bulk of body to send to wash room. This was result of long sleep and heavy diet which continued throughout day. She was a happy self looking and considered self symbol of sound health. She didn't like boney face or structure. Even Elizabeth Tailor was criticized for slim and shapely body. She only imitated fashion tips from them which appeared in magazines. Ratan loved to see half covered bodies and enjoyed and never expected any such thing from wife. He only feared sickness of wife which doubled or trebled his workload. She had regular bouts of headaches when she behaved like arrogant and lost temper and rolled on bed for hours. He applied balm repeatedly and she took number of pills spoiling lever functioning. She was convinced by doctor with difficulty and after getting admitted in hospital for one month for different treatments unheard by him. He murmured on loss of hard earned money through carelessness.

In fact after marriage he acquired knowledge about good health followed by articles on net about symptoms and also simple treatments which she never believed. Ratan at times wanted to slap wife for idiotic actions, but never did so imagining scene which could emerge afterwards. It must be true with all educated husbands who tolerated their ill behaved counterparts.

3

All experiences turned Ratan into docile husband and he finally accepted control by wife. His old behavior returned when he ignored all words spoken and did everything of liking making wife crazy. He walked out on plea of meeting friends. He returned after few hours of loitering disliked by his peace loving self and entered house as a timid person showing grief on face. Ratan felt satisfied by own act which brought some loving and caressing from roaring lioness and also some good food, which she prepared well when resolved to do so. This treat was enough for him to spend a few months bearing any or all types of rough treatments. He definitely thanked his good luck for this pleasant time intermittently.

Ratan thought, "Does higher education make a person numb and submissive to greater extent? Or is it an effective pill to keep mind intoxicated with knowledge when smaller actions don't make any impact? Or is it that man becomes highly self occupied not to notice things happening around? In other words he becomes nonexistent before his dear ones." It was good that his intelligent wife didn't analyze in this manner which could make life more troublesome. Ratan concentrated on his work and never bothered to correct himself in anyway. Life went on peacefully and they made few friends for socializing. This normalized his tense conjugal life. This also was not enough. One day wife came back in morning after walk in which she tried to meet people to give long lecture, "How someone can gossip for long that too in standing position." He knew her habit who always tried to lie down on sofa instead of sitting. Funniest part was that she didn't mind to do so even in presence of outsiders. While shifting her legs she never bothered about glimpses available to guests. She didn't bother as long Ratan was available to fight with person taking wrong views. She reported about morning gossip which was a long narration. The gist of which was, "Today I met a couple walking very slow and who stopped every ten minutes. This was good for me when they talked nicely and shared experiences. Husband underwent three times heart surgery to clear blocked arteries. His zeal to live was extraordinary. You can't believe she is wife of a retired doctor and seventy years of age, much elder to me. They still eat well and also dozens of medicines. Both were sporting and encouraging. They walked regularly and also toured to places leaving working son and wife free to spend time. Financially they kept independent."

"Why are you giving these details? How will this help us? Few minutes back you looked gloomy and tired and now you have bloomed." Ratan couldn't check asking despite knowing her rude behavior.

"This is problem with you not to accept my words and consider me a slow witted person never understanding what is being said. You forget that last time in ladies club I won first prize for public speaking and all praised my intelligence for days together. Even now ladies keep asking how to prepare for delivering good speech before learned audience. Few have benefitted by my wise words and guidance and gave treat after getting success." Ratan didn't remember any such thing happening but kept silent not to extend discussion. He wanted to get ready for college which sometimes was liked by Sita. He could get rid of her after many more talks releasing frustration in all areas of life particularly post retirement when she didn't find enough money to spend. It often reflected in activities in bed. She didn't realize that advanced age doesn't allow frequent indulgence. She suffered with high blood pressure for years and was always under risk. She preferred rich diets to satisfy taste bud. Ratan patiently carried on not to invite serious damage to self and wife although no doctor ever said clearly.

One day again she met Ms Gawain whose husband retired as VP from a private firm and immediately bought a luxury segment car, a symbol of high status. Sita couldn't digest this and was after Ratan to change old car with a sedan model so that she may feel higher status and impress friends. She also wanted him to keep driver so that she could do marketing or visit relations living in city during day when he was in college. He agreed to first proposal of buying new car by exchanging old one, but didn't deploy driver. He wanted to drive so that physical alertness remained intact. He had seen retired Presidents in US and India driving own car and also kept trim and fit. He never considered driving inferior. It is only in this country people find driving inferior activity and having drivers a status symbol.

Ratan as his habit was decided on new Tata Model bigger size which pleased Sita like dream coming true. She hugged husband when he came first day in car and went on long drive of twenty kilometers and offered dinner with red wine to celebrate occasion. She took excess quantity and Ratan had difficulty to calm her down and she reported sick next morning. Ratan had to make breakfast and left some for wife before leaving for college. She declared to sleep long and didn't open door to maid in morning as usual. The routine got upset and house was cleaned up only next day. Maid talked, "It seems you went for drink party yesterday to celebrate for new car. I should get sweets as customary treat." Ratan accepted behavior of wife blindly. This type acting helped him to keep nerve cool and pay attention to work. It proved comfortable for him as he could manage with low budget. She spoke many words of praise and also many good wishes for growth and prosperity. It's easy to extract good utterances from such people like maids with less expense which are very comforting.

Next moment she changed color, "You have changed and don't love me considering old and cold. You should have picked me up from bed after hugging. This is simplest expression of love for wife."

"You get ready and then discuss." Ratan said smiling.

Sita went inside and came back to hug husband for long. She found written with red lipstick on mirror, "Sita my dearest I love you so much."

Ratan rushed to lift not to be delayed and keep his reputation in adhering to time.

Pushed to Live

1

Sandak and Mani also came to take a dip in River in Orissa on this pious occasion and pay homage in to ancestors who died earlier many years ago. It was a ritual to remember them to keep legacy of life like many other religions round globe. This was typical in this part of world. People kept fast for many days and ate only after taking bath in river and worship with water in hand. They chanted some Sanskrit verses while dropping water back into stream. Water was cool in this time of year and gave shiver to standing people in stream which was having strong current. Not very far off river dropped below many hundred feet. Every year mishaps took place and men, women and children were getting drowned and died. Dipali also stood in water by side of parents holding hand of Sandak not to get swept away. Administration was alert particularly on this occasion when millions of people visited this place for couple of days. Other arrangements were also made like parking of vehicles, stalls for food and also for items required to worship god in temple on bank of river. Temple looked to be hundreds of years old but was maintained well to show its upkeep. Many rich people donated huge amounts of money which was kept by trust and head priest lived a lavish life. There were other deities in temples but least worshiped like differentiation in families in real life. It was nostalgic in many respects and one could enjoy this bath if coming only for touring. Certain freshness in body and inner self was enjoyed by one and all and they ate good and tasty dishes being sold in shops. Mostly people spent days to see magnificent evening Aarti of river and also avail romantic time, particularly newlywed who turned up in many numbers. Sandak entered water slowly and looked at Mani with lust forgetting the religious part. He held her closely and neglected young daughter who was attracted to a boy. They were taking bath together and expressed their liking for each other. It was not his first touch with young Dipali. He enjoyed intimacy with many in college when acting in plays. This was first time he felt different and both walked inside a store to buy gifts for each other. "No you may select first and I shall look for something else for my younger brother as a birthday gift," replied Dipali.

There were a few exchanges and lastly invitation for a cup of coffee was extended. This brief introduction developed into a close friendship and finally in marriage tie for life. Mani knew this development after many months when Dipali reported about pregnancy one night when she became very sick. They searched for boy but didn't find him. It was too late to get rid of pregnancy and finally she became unwed mother. Sandak and Mani moved out from old town and found job in city where such abnormalities were accepted with less criticism; rather none bothered about affairs and life of others. All met in formal manners and wished happiness without bothering much for any truthfulness in statements. Mani was daughter of a clerk in municipal office with modest income to run family. She was only daughter and became a spoiled one like many of her friends. She was flirting with many temporary friends. Sandak was one who got married to her due to his temperament. Many days he served wife when she complained of body pain and he rarely missed chances to fulfill his lust. Sandak was son of senior officer in government and managed to convince parents for marriage; who themselves were married without consent of parents. It took them long to come back into family and forced to stay for years in isolation. Mani already conceived which made parents to surrender for happiness of son.

Sandak and Mani entered home in absence of father under direction of mother. That was a typical one act play when wife allured husband and sent them in front of father in morning standing by their side. Husband got signal and blessed new couple without delay. In fact his mother also married father like this only and was an inter-caste marriage. The family had long history of love marriages and often quoted by neighbors and acquaintances. Their life remained always happy. Sandak and Mani spent few days with parents and returned back to their quarter to save job. Such thing never happened with daughter and she became burden for parents bringing up newly born son. Dipali decided to work and picked up a job in a local store as sales girl. She was free from feeding child and it was left to mother. Child grew well and looked charming. Family became more distorted day by day.

Cross cultural life settings have their own woos which couples and family members bear as many adjustments are required. Main constraint being limited social circle as many persons don't entertain these trend setters and always feel it to be against social norms. Modernization might bring many conveniences, but mental blocks don't vanish till some liberalized norms grow up in society. Education facilitates but is not a cure for such limited approach in conservative society.

2

Dharam was son of Dipali who completed law degree and started practicing in town bar council and became famous criminal lawyer. He charged high fees and never gave any concession to anyone. His wife Nishi worked full time in political party office and dreamed becoming head of state. Now they were not dependent on mother or grandparents.

Dipali one day came to their residence after knowing his success as advocate and was welcomed. He firstly got shock to see dress of mother which was hiding her real age. She looked more fashionable than wife. But Nishi never showed any complex about this. Dipali didn't like dressing of daughter-in-law and later understood reason when explained.

Chandrakant was her boyfriend who ditched and ran away after sleeping with her. She was victim of uncontrolled emotion at young age. Now she wanted to file suit for compensation. Dharam didn't agree for this as it was difficult to get justice in such cases. His mother would face an ordeal of extraordinary insult and humiliation, which he couldn't bear. Chandrakant was Collector of district and a powerful man and stayed in town. It was difficult to sue him in court on flimsy ground and without any substantive proof. Court looked for concrete evidence and not a story to punish anyone. Secondly mother carried on her immoral act and gave birth to him. It was going to be his insult also.

He would lose reputation in society. Dharam was puzzled but clear about his action.

Mother was not having good reputation to his knowledge and decided not to give publicity to being son of such woman. She was reputed for overtures in her company and made friends to have pleasant time including her boss who frequented her place in odd hours. It was known to neighbors and everyone kept distance from her. Dharam was demoralized and went out of town for a month. Nishi stayed and gave normal respect to mother. She was having sympathy as to her knowledge hundreds face such ordeals who came to her for redresses, compensation and other favors.

3

Dipali also lived in shock for many days and spent time in drinking and sleeping for long hours. She worked out a plan to trap Chandrakant in a plot and insult him. She found out one old friend who could take her in house of Chandrakant.

"My father has been issued a warrant of arrest for murder of a worker who was working in our factory for many years. He is innocent and the man died in accident. He was trapped into running conveyor belt in night hours when trying to clean the chute where material was discharged. He was sleepy and the steel rod used to clean was trapped in belt which dragged him inside and he got crushed. Doctor has also given this report. Father was in house when accident happened. But union man has complained and got issued warrant." Dipali told Chandrakant.

"Why your father has not come so that I could talk to him and find out details? Please ask him to come."

"What type of man are you who don't want to help man in distress? This won't be appreciated by anyone in society," said Dipali.

"I think we should come with your father and talk. This will be fair and quick." Her friend said.'You don't know this man. He allured me many years back after promising to marry and never returned. I became unwed mother. My parents were kind to shelter me. He can't understand ordeal that I faced before society and we have come to this place.' Dipali said.

'You are talking nonsense. I don't know you and never met you anytime before. Don't try to rob my prestige?' Collector became tough now.

Nishi came to see collector with some work, which was routine matter of administration. She was given due respect by him and offered a seat.

'Why are you here? Collector is a busy man and you are disturbing him.' Nishi told Dipali. She explained how Dipali was related to her and has been talking about some incident when you came in contact with her at young age. But don't mind. It could be a mistake. She has recognized wrong person and blaming unnecessarily. My husband also didn't like her behavior and has left home for a month to get rid from her.'She is carrying memory of father at the age of five years and lost them in a caste riot and got shelter in an orphanage. Riot was due to an incident of a higher caste boy having relationship. Someone saw them together when girl was trying to get away. Two groups fought and many got injured. The case was hushed up by police without any action and deaths were never reported which included her father.' Nishi made new story.

Dipali got furious and walked out without even taking friend with her. She now knew that getting fair treatment here was difficult. She quit job and lived in isolation. After serious dejection she became abnormal and was admitted in mental hospital by Dharam. Nishi visited her at intervals.

Dharam left practicing law after some days when his mother became abnormal. He developed hatred for society and left wife alone and vanished. He became rebellious and gathered goons to loot people and enjoy life. He also brought women in his group to participate. He met villagers and addressed them in strong words to make them rebellious. His group became renowned for atrocities which increased when he remembered mother in mental hospital. He provoked them to revolt against establishments.

4

Nishi became a prominent leader in state and fought elections and became Cabinet Minister. She was against ways her husband wanted to bring changes. This was her third term and was considered very sensible and reasonable leader making peace wherever any disturbance happened. She was elected to Central Committee of party which was deciding policies. Many members differed on issues and she was charged with corruption in a project in her area. She monitored this project personally. Finally she was cleared from charges after enquiry and she became more powerful and candidate for next Chief Minister from party.

She led the party to victory with good margin and was elected leader to become CM. This was a big day and Dipali came to congratulate her. She recovered and was now a changed person. She was given room in outhouse to live and got food from the mess being run for visitors to CM every day. One day Dipali thought "How this transformation happened and why her son became an armed rebel from advocate? Perhaps they got influenced by Chinese Revolution of "Power through Nozzle of Guns".

She had no liability and her husband left her alone. She didn't know where about or detail of his activities. Some persons informed about Dharam being in deep forest with poor and ferocious villagers who had taken to arms to fight showing anguish for their poor condition. In this process they damaged schools, blew up many bridges and disrupted movement of people and forces. It became difficult for moving law and order reinforcement and made them bold to do anything they wanted. They also killed forces by planting underground mines on roads. Dharam was deeply involved in conspiracies which initially he guided from nearby city or town. Now he was followed by police in forest for several crimes committed by his group. He acted against government agencies. His life changed and he was on self styled exile. He grew big bushy beard and started using khaki dresses and long shirt with pajama and carried carbine. He could manage without many dresses. He used to take dip in water pool or in streams naked and used dress made from leaves till clothes dried. His daily routine was not fixed and didn't know what to eat and where. His group used to collect food from village shop and he paid them to earn their sympathy. Those young persons, shopkeepers and many school teachers from villages acted as informers. School teachers helped in distribution of pamphlets and printed messages in villages. Late evening male members, young boys and girls assembled and heard his speeches regarding ideology and forced them to join movement from homes. The influence was growing fast and many young boys and girls joined as volunteers and trained in arms operations. Some of them were trained in sophisticated arms which emboldened them and they planned more activities. Dharam became Supreme Commander. One morning Dharam was getting ready in a lonely place in Jungle when he was shot dead from behind by a gunman from own group. He abused him for being selfish and taking all money. The person was second in command and none opposed his action. They silently took body and threw in pool of water in forest for animals to feast. They moved away and left the present area and locate in other place.

5

Anna and Niki were not allowed to get married and went into a temple against wishes of parents and registered by priest on a stamp paper. This was legally acceptable. Thereafter they met parents forcing them to accept. Both continued their education up to graduation with average result which could have employed them as clerks. Mother said, "You won't do a job now anytime in future."

"Alright I will be a house maker only." She accepted command as mark of respect. Anna studied to compete in administrative services examination. They wanted to show determination again and wife supported his efforts.

She worked hard to make him comfortable. Niki did all housekeeping jobs and gave relief to mother-in-law. Father-in-law was also happy. Mother frequently visited relations and attended social and religious programs.

"Are you happy with us? You shouldn't hesitate in asking anything required and I shall be happy to give the same," once father told.

"Papa we are very happy. Kindly bless us so that Anna is successful in examination and make you proud," replied Niki.

"He will definitely succeed. Your mother is not here but she will also be happy with his success," father assured.

Anna appeared in examination and was successful. Niki was happy with his rank of successful candidates and was joined Police Services. He happily accepted this. He was happy to see wife's pleasure. Now mother relented as her daughter-in-law was staying at home. She organized special get together before he left to join his service and invited all friends and relatives residing in nearby places. This was a very solemn occasion for whole family and society gave special recognition. The day of departure was very painful for mother and wife. Mother wept severely. Niki was upset but controlled to show greater maturity and not to disturb husband.

Anna worked hard during training to do well and get good cadre. He concentrated in the training and ranked higher as desired. He was posted to a district full of Naxalite activities. He started working and now lived with family in government quarters along with parents. "You know what attracts me most? These are your sweet face and thick lips." Two enjoyed conjugal life freely. Niki became pregnant within few months. All were happy and two were more concerned for child expected after sometime. Anna wanted to be posted in headquarter but this couldn't happen.

Son was born and mother assisted daughter-in-law in caring of baby. They celebrated birth of child which was attended by parents of Niki. They gifted money and a house to grandchild which was accepted by family after some resistance.

Anna was an efficient officer and controlled situations quickly. He got little time to see Soma staying with mother. He was made in charge of group specially trained to control Naxalite and frequently faced encounters. He was killed in one of these when Soma was hardly three years old. Family went into distress."Mother I would now get into job and take revenge of Anna. You allow me to compete in examination," Niki told mother.

"Yes you must do this and I will take care of your son." Mother replied firmly. Niki got enrolled for competitive examination and started working hard. She was a brilliant student and could prepare without difficulty. Her devotion was impressive which forced parents of Anna to take complete care of family. They didn't face problem of money as Anna received money in compensation from government.

Niki competed in first chance and also got very good rank. She was posted in Capital and started working in Home Ministry after a stint of two years in state.

All these days she paid least attention to son who now became very serious as small boy. He did everything and never took help from mother or grandparents.

"If all children could be trained like this, no parents will face difficulty in caring of a child. Self discipline is inculcated from family and learning become natural and confidence building." Niki thought while patting Soma in bed. Motherly feelings returned and devotion to work intensified. She earned fame in short time. Niki developed friendship with ladies and formed a forum to educate them on Sundays for a few hours. It was a bad day for Niki when she was informed by school authorities that Soma was missing from school after lunch. He was playing in ground and someone allured him to take home informing about grandmother's illness. Niki couldn't think about such happening with her son as they spent very peaceful life. She was having reputation of a fair and just person. She was in ladies center and immediately rushed home. She didn't lose her head and set in search of child silently and informed police chief to act. She wept in night without letting anyone know. All were astonished on her extraordinary courage. She was depending only on mercy of god.

6

Niki avoided publicity about disappearance of her son and kept away from media. She thought publicity could endanger life of son as they churn stories to maximum for making business and attract audiences in larger numbers. Despite prevailing rules and restrictions they indulged in this process. Many times it became obvious that media was misusing freedom to make life of general public torturous and difficult. Media in fact followed no social ethics in working. Young reporters also dwelt on many subjects and issues without acquiring valid information. They tried to copy other competing media person for scoring high. They altered some details which were threatening fragmented society. There was a free play and picked up viewers from street who gave careless and irresponsible opinions and biased views.

Niki's parents came to know about abduction and didn't talk after being forbidden by her. Administrative Cadre was more concerned and never allowed matters to blow out of proportion. They waited someone to demand ransom to release abducted child. This was not happening in this case. This was a surprise for many in administration while Niki tried to connect incidents to happenings in past some time. One name occurred to mind was name of Ranjit who was absconding from gang and was hiding with a lady Mitali who declared self as police agent following the man. This was a very popular story making rounds.

'See any use of force may precipitate the issue seriously and life of child would get endangered. Persons have done it to take revenge for some difficulties they might have faced due to strictness in administration. This is a gray area of job I am doing. But I have to act in interest of people in general who can't be allowed to suffer for wrong deeds of some vested interest. Otherwise also terrorism or destruction has become general trend to force issues on government.' Niki explained to in-laws.'Those who express their sympathies instantly may not be true. This also is a face saving way to survive and continue to disturb. Our political system is mainly at fault. Social norms have distorted. Society has become a self maneuvering place for personal gains. This has become major consideration and humanity has been put on back burner.' She emphasized."We may progress materialistically and become moneyed. But we are bound to lose peace of mind and get internally disturbed. This many times forces abnormal and unwanted behavior.' She talked further.'This incident is manifestation of abnormal mind. This is a type of remorseful satisfaction trying to harm one or other. When this becomes a destructive; action like exploding a bomb in crowded place, trains, market or public gathering is nothing but creating terror to restrict free movement of people. All are copying acts of celluloid heroes. This is no way related to real life. All blame administration for problems they face.' Niki sounded highly perturbed. Family was unable to accept these words and showed disturbance on their faces. They were constantly praying god who could only save child. They remained in poor state of mind and paid special attention not to talk anything in public despite provocations. They still awaited demand for ransom which never came and days passed. Niki wept in nights alone and worked normal in day time. She was missing support of her brave husband. All were surprised to see this courageous lady and mother and appreciated.

7

The group which was responsible for abduction was Royal Sena. Dharam was already dead but this didn't come to public knowledge. Ranjit took over the group and became active. His Royal Sena went to loot a bank for getting money to pay for arms supplied from neighboring country. Action was planned and executed by Rawat, second man in command. Who was more brutal in action and planned many severe and damaging activities. He was having bad reputation. None dared to oppose.

Once this group was challenged by villagers from nearby area when Ranjit was injured severely and had to run away to save life. He was hospitalized in unknown locality. This hospital was run by Senior Area Commander of Sena who was highly educated. He was respected and generally appreciated for social activities and helping children in education. He picked up some notorious and brave children to be trained for the group by Sena.

They failed in looting bank as security forces got alerted by informer who watched movement of group. In frustration they picked up son of Commander of security forces pointed out by their man in public who was cadre member. He was a local politician who failed to get elected in last election. "What is your name?" Ranjit asked

"My mother is District Magistrate. My father died fighting terrorists few years back. I was in school and playing during lunch break when uncle picked me up to take to hospital to see my sick grandfather. But he brought me here." She told fearlessly.

Ranjit was moved and asked one man to take child to school and leave him there. The principal informed Niki about return of child. No detail could be given by them. Son narrated story himself and mother accepted without questions. The police reported about member of Sena bringing back child to school. Niki didn't respond to any question by press. Niki knew that terrorists worked for leaders during election to create fear in minds of half educated public and praised by leaders for their political consciousness in many words. They also paid enough money in turn for ensuring future support. She avoided publicity of incident and took risk of losing her only son. She only believed on God for help." She was cool.

Random Love

1

Strong hailstorm was just over. It came suddenly from nowhere and town was in pitch dark condition. Wind was blowing at very high speed and it seemed all houses and trees would come down to earth. People ran for shelter in different places. Traffic came to halt and all rickshaws were left under tree and men went inside nearest hotel sheds. Some running cars were forced to stop as visibility was almost zero. Even cars were left in middle of roads and owners preferred to save their lives rather than vehicle. Some drivers parked cars away from trees for safety but kept sitting inside as they couldn't get time to move out. Many chanted Om Shanti and prayed lord Siva for protecting from this storm. Suddenly storm stopped and within no time town became alive as if some magic happened.

Ravi sat in a pensive mood sitting in a lonely place on the bank of holy river which was his passion whenever he visited this place. He has been staying here for last one week and roaming in the street. He also faced storm which was just over and recalled something similar brooding inside his mind and heart. His college was closed and he developed habit of passing time like this only. There was fresh air and lovely food was available even in ordinary eatery and was tasty and better than cooked by his servant. Ramu was also granted leave for many days and allowed to enjoy. The boys working around were busy not to see any customer's face. Orders for food were controlled and supplied by them through some intuition as they never made any mistake in billing. Desk was occupied by a young girl who was called Deepa by elders owning food joint just left side.

Deepa was dark complexioned and with smiling face. He could judge her cleavages when she walked as if moving on ramp in a fashion parade. Her sharp features could allure anyone without fail. Her voice was rough and sounded manly. Nature creates variations just to keep men and women entangled often without attachments. But at times I love it happens that man falls in love unknowingly and suddenly. Similar was coincident now when Deepa passed by Ravi and her body brushed with his back while sitting on bench.

'What you like to eat? I find no boy is asking you since long. As for you, you seem to be dumb seeing around people coming and going.' She asked him.

'I am like this only. I am professor in college and greatly tired of talking. These day students want to be dictated subject matter and never buy books. Many like to download from net on computer and others photo copy from library books. Constant explaining is required to make them pass examinations in general.'

'And you get tired of doing this.' Deepa completed his statement.

'You look to be very intelligent.' Ravi complimented.

'You are right. I am gold medalist in history from university. My professor was just like you in look and posture. He also kept silence after class and rarely talked to students or other teachers. You don't look like scholar.' Deepa commented.

'You look scholar even while working in this food shop. Your posture also gives such impression. How are you able to make money? You must be under debt by now.' Ravi answered.

'You are absolutely wrong. My sales have been growing every month. More persons are coming to eat here. I give them personal care and keep boys on toes.' She retorted.

'I don't think so. Do you keep accounts to show me truth in what you claimed right now?' He asked.

'Why should I show you my accounts? Are you from sales tax or any such department who are given work of harassing shopkeeper?' She was angry now.

'Now you look like fool. Moments back I told you about me being professor and still you are questioning my work.' He retorted.

'Then you are a dull teacher who doesn't know what he is talking about.' She replied hurriedly.

'Sorry madam, I have never met such dull sales person anytime. I won't eat here now and going to next shop.' Ravi got up to go.

One elderly man walked to intervene, 'This is why I told you not to come here in shop. You will drive all clients away by your arguments. Here people come to eat and listen to your lecture. You are better in your college.' Jagdeep told daughter.

2

Ravi stayed back and pitied woman who was looking foolish now. Her real identity was disclosed. She interacted with Ravi for self entertainment and not being attracted to him. He now looked doomed and his myth about girl was gone. He combed his hair with all fingers, rubbed his head vigorously and shook heavily. He wanted to throw out all imagination and come to realities of life. He had suffered already a lot and didn't want to continue. Now he realized life doesn't run with emotions and realities must be applied. He also felt that picturesque place was just for temporary period. He must find a substantive life partner who could work hard with him. His objective was to write a thesis on "How religion is deceptive and making one crippled to be effective." This could only be possible if very strong woman could become his life partner. He instantly got up and walked fast towards city not bothering for any vehicle. His pace was fast that anyone could doubt him to be abnormal. On turning he collided with a young girl of twenty who held her from falling. She didn't grudge and looked on his face.

"What's hurry and why you are running? Are you being chased by someone after you have picked up valuables of lady on bank of river?" Girl questioned directly.

"No. Why you are questioning like police officer?" Ravi asked in return.

"I am Inspector of police of this area. Just now I received a call of theft. Now you have to come with me as you are under doubt." Rekha said and took him to police station.

Ravi thought this was realism and now it will take a few hours to convince inspector before getting released. He lost every dream and now looking to the lockup in one corner of the place. There were three persons who looked criminal by face and dress. He started imagining how he would adjust with them inside cell. He wanted to run away somehow when Rekha got busy with staff gathering reports since morning. She was on round till morning and came back on duty after resting a while and without eating anything. Mother pressed for eating and she didn't pay attention and rushed on foot. Police station was not far from her quarter.

She got free and now looked at Ravi. She intently looked on his face which was full of worry. A feeling of sympathy passed through her and she made sound of 'chu..chu..chu.' and smiled mildly. Ravi saw her making this sound and thought about tough time.

"Ravi sir. Why are you looking so sad? I am your student and now working in police as told by you. You thought woman are not fit to work in police. Now you can see I am here before you. My grip was strong and you couldn't get free from it. That proves I have physical strength too. Do you agree?"

Ravi shook his head telling yes but didn't speak a word. He was unable to think what to talk to her. Rekha ordered breakfast for self and Ravi.

"This is my fee to you for opening my mind. Please forgive me for utterances what I made after holding you. I watched you since last two days on bank of river and ascertained identity. Today I came out early to meet you on river side only and found you near my house. Does this mean anything to you?"

Ravi again shook his head in negative. He was not able to comprehend situation and find words to respond. He felt insulted first and now he was earning respect from this woman. Rekha forced him to eat which he obeyed. Thereafter she took him to her quarter and introduced to mother.

"He is my professor Ravi who emboldened me after I became without father. You became disturbed and kept crying all time. He encouraged me to get into job and I got selected in first chance. Training of police was tough and painful but I didn't care and passed through all tests. I got first rank and became Inspector quickly. This was his entire gift."

3

Ravi was still not talking and looking at faces of confident duo. He looked around and found their living quite satisfactory. Idea flashed into his mind if Rekha agreed to be his wife, he would be a happy person. She can shake out any irrelevant thoughts from my head and make me happy. Now he heard Rekha asking mother.

"Will you accept professor your son-in-law? I want to marry him."

"Are you mad? We have to confirm first from him." Mother replied.

"Don't worry he is going to say yes. Otherwise also he has been caught by this inspector and wouldn't like to go to lockup and then to jail." Rekha talked boldly.

"I am agreeable and don't want to be jailed. It's better to be here in your jail. But I am must be allowed to go to do teaching work after two weeks when classes are starting." Ravi said.

"We also don't want to feed you all time. You must earn and feed your wife like others. You must buy dresses, ornaments to use during long holidays. We will plan trips to distant places and mother won't be there." Rekha spoke quickly.

"You have gone mad. These talks are done by guardian and not by bride. You have talked enough and keep shut." Mother told daughter. Rekha became silent.

Further discussion took place and finally marriage ceremony was held in house of Rekha. Her relatives participated and Ravi had none to be present. He stayed in their house for a week and then came back to his quarter in his town and became busy in teaching. Rekha talked to him regularly taking his care. She was now vey sweet voiced and never talked like inspector. Ravi understood that life can turn faster than imagined. He was now a responsible and happy person glued to one own family and could share thoughts with mother. Mother was very affectionate and Ravi forgot all his pains and gloomy time.

Printed in the United States
By Bookmasters